"We're not talking about a real marriage," she assured him. "It would be a marriage on paper."

She was desperate, Rick realized. So desperate she was on the verge of tears. Walking away from Megan Ford would be hard to do. He'd be haunted forever by those big blue eyes.

"What kind of coffee do you make?"

She blinked several times. "What kind? I—I usually grind my own beans. I like—"

"Grind your own beans? Tell me you can cook, too."

Megan gave him a befuddled stare. "Well, yes. Of course."

He grinned at her, hoping to chase away those tears that still lingered. "Honey, looks like we got a deal."

* * *

Come back to Cactus, Texas, in Judy Christenberry's bestselling series TOTS FOR TEXANS! You're guaranteed to have a grand ole time!

Dear Reader,

Spring is coming with all its wonderful scents and colors, and here at Harlequin American Romance we've got a wonderful bouquet of romances to please your every whim!

Few women can refuse a good bargain, but what about a sexy rancher who needs a little help around the house? Wait till you hear the deal Megan Ford offers Rick Astin in Judy Christenberry's *The Great Texas Wedding Bargain*, the continuation of her beloved miniseries TOTS FOR TEXANS!

Spring is a time for new life, and no one blossoms more beautifully than a woman who's WITH CHILD.... In *That's Our Baby!*, the first book in this heartwarming new series, Pamela Browning travels to glorious Alaska to tell the story of an expectant mother and the secret father of her child.

Then we have two eligible bachelors whose fancies turn not lightly, but rather unexpectedly, to thoughts of love. Don't miss *The Cowboy and the Countess*, Darlene Scalera's tender story about a millionaire who has no time for love until a bump on the head brings his childhood sweetheart back into his life. And in Rita Herron's *His-and-Hers Twins*, single dad Zeke Blalock is showered with wife candidates when his little girls advertise for a mother...but only one special woman will do!

So this March, don't forget to stop and smell the roses—and enjoy all four of our wonderful Harlequin American Romance titles!

Happy reading!

Melissa Jeglinski
Associate Senior Editor

The Great Texas Wedding Bargain

JUDY CHRISTENBERRY

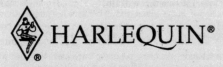

HARLEQUIN®

TORONTO • NEW YORK • LONDON
AMSTERDAM • PARIS • SYDNEY • HAMBURG
STOCKHOLM • ATHENS • TOKYO • MILAN • MADRID
PRAGUE • WARSAW • BUDAPEST • AUCKLAND

ISBN 0-373-16817-9

THE GREAT TEXAS WEDDING BARGAIN

Copyright © 2000 by Judy Christenberry.

Visit us at www.romance.net

Printed in U.S.A.

ABOUT THE AUTHOR

Judy Christenberry has been writing romances for fifteen years because she loves happy endings as much as her readers. Judy quit teaching French recently to devote her time to writing. She hopes readers have as much fun reading her stories as she does writing them. She spends her spare time reading, watching her favorite sports teams and keeping track of her two daughters. Judy's a native Texan, living in Plano, a suburb of Dallas.

Books by Judy Christenberry

HARLEQUIN AMERICAN ROMANCE

*4 Brides for 4 Brothers
#4 Tots for 4 Texans

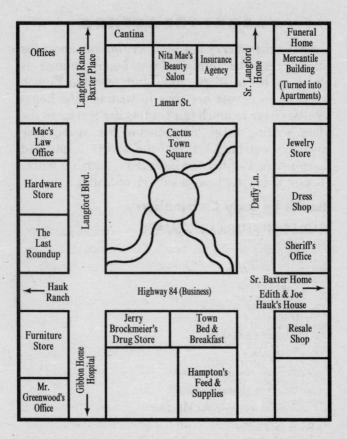

Chapter One

He was the one.

Megan Ford nibbled on her bottom lip as she stared at the dusty cowboy leaning against the feed-store counter. She'd heard Mr. James, the store owner, call him by name, confirming his identity.

Richard Astin.

Her mother's friends had recommended him.

If she weren't so desperate… But she was. Time was of the essence.

"Well, hello, there, Megan. What can I do for you?" Mr. James called out, having finally seen her in the dim shadows of the store.

"Good afternoon, Mr. James." She remembered he'd gone to school with her mother and treated her as if she were a favorite niece even though she'd only met him a month ago.

The cowboy turned around to glance at her, and she sucked in a deep breath. He might appear tired, dirty and down-at-the-heels, but he was good-looking. Maybe he wasn't as perfect for her plans as she'd thought. But she didn't have any other candidates.

She stepped forward and extended her hand to the stranger. "I don't think I've met you. I'm Megan Ford."

"Sorry, I should've introduced you," Mr. James said. "This here is Richard Astin. We call him Rick. He's got a smart little spread outside of town."

She smiled politely. "How nice."

His eyebrows raised over his warm brown eyes. "Yeah. Are you ranching in the area?"

She shook her head. "No, I'm a nurse. I work for the doctors." She didn't need to give their names. Dr. Greenfield had been the only doctor in the west Texas town of Cactus for a number of years. He'd recently taken in a partner, Samantha Gibbons. She'd married one of the local men last summer.

The cowboy didn't look terribly interested in her history. Even better.

Turning back to Mr. James, the cowboy finished his business and started to go, tipping his hat at her as he strode past.

She wanted to grab his sleeve, to stop his departure, but she certainly didn't want to conduct a conversation in front of Mr. James. That would never do.

With a quick nod in the older man's direction, she followed Richard Astin outside.

"Mr. Astin?" she called out. He'd covered a lot

of territory in the two minutes he'd been out of her sight and was now standing at the door of an old pickup.

"Yes, ma'am?"

In the sunlight, though his gaze was shaded by his cowboy hat, the strong planes of his face were visible, making Megan hesitate. He wouldn't be easy to manipulate.

She drew a deep breath. It was now or never. "Could I have a word with you?"

RICHARD ASTIN stared at the pretty woman on the porch of the feed store.

Not another one.

He'd thought he was safe here in Cactus. The eight months since he'd moved here had been the happiest of his life. The good people of Cactus took a man at face value…and left him to live in peace.

Well, most of them. The Matchmakers weren't quite as good about staying out of a man's life. But he'd found them amusing. The four women had gotten their sons married, with children on the way. Then they had started looking for fresh bait. But lately they'd left him alone.

"Yes, ma'am? Talk to me about whàt?" He didn't budge. She could come to him. Maybe there was another dance and the ladies had sent her over to lure him to it.

His left eyebrow was raised as he recognized distress on her face. Those blue eyes of hers appeared wary and she was nibbling on her full bottom lip.

She took one step toward him, and stopped. "It's...it's personal."

He dipped his head down so she wouldn't see his grin. He wondered which matchmaker had put her up to approaching him. He'd have to tell them that she didn't know much about flirting.

Looking up, he said, "Can't be too personal. We just met."

"Could I buy you a cup of coffee?"

Now she was tempting him. He'd never learned to make good coffee. The instant kind he made each morning was only a mockery of the fragrant coffee he loved. "Where?"

His question seemed to throw her. She should've planned better. He could give her pointers, from his past experiences, but why help the enemy?

"At the drugstore?"

He deliberately looked at his watch. No point in letting her think she'd roped him in. "I've got five minutes to spare."

Her chin rose. "Then we'd better walk fast," she retorted and turned on her heel to head down the sidewalk in the direction of Brockmeier's Drugstore.

Rick chuckled under his breath. At least she had some spirit. She'd been so hesitant at first, he'd thought she was timid.

He strolled after her, not hurrying, but his long legs caught up with her a few storefronts away. Not that she had short legs. Her denim skirt ended above her knees, catching his eye.

No doubt she was good-looking. Half the single men in town should be after her. He didn't understand why she was chasing him. Unless she knew his secret.

She stopped outside the drugstore and turned to make sure he'd followed. He'd admired her restraint in not looking before. He reached around her and held open the door.

Sweeping past him with her chin raised, in the fashion of a grand duchess, she headed for the side of the drugstore where several empty booths awaited customers.

"Howdy, Rick," Lucy, the waitress, called out. Then she noticed the young woman standing beside him. "Megan, right? You're Faith's daughter. Welcome to town."

"Thank you. May we sit anywhere?"

Lucy waved them toward the booths. "You bet, hon. Take your pick. It's not like we're busy."

Rick followed Megan's determined march and slid into the booth she chose, opposite her.

"What can I get you folks?" Lucy asked.

"A cup of coffee for the gentleman and iced tea for me. Would you care for anything else, Mr. Astin? I believe the pie is supposed to be good."

"Best in town," Lucy declared, staring at Rick, waiting for his decision.

He deliberately took his time, watching Megan's antsy movements across from him. "What kind do you have?"

"Apple, coconut cream and chocolate."

"I'll have apple, with a scoop of ice cream," he said, smiling at Lucy.

"Coming right up."

"For someone who only has five minutes, you're certainly taking your time," Megan muttered as Lucy hurried away from their table.

"Pie's worth the extra time," he assured her, adding a wink. He thought she seemed a little tense, but it was silly to get her tail in such a twist over a dance.

She glared at him.

"Look, honey, don't act so uptight. If going to a dance is that important, I'll take you." This time he might even enjoy himself.

Her blue eyes widened and she blinked several times. "I beg your pardon?"

"That's what you wanted, isn't it? To ask me to take you to a dance? I'll have to admit, buying me pie and coffee is a new approach. I like it."

Her mouth dropped open. A tasty little mouth, too. Full lips, slightly pink, no lipstick. In fact, she didn't have on hardly any makeup at all. Most of the women who'd come after him usually loaded up on the war paint.

Smart lady. Her dark lashes framed her blue eyes and her cheeks were soft pink over ivory. She didn't need any fake enhancements.

"Why, you conceited...conceited oaf!" she exclaimed.

He gave her a lopsided grin. "Did I get it wrong? Okay, what *do* you want? We don't know each other. I doubt you'd want to buy cows. I can't think of any other business we'd have.''

She suddenly retreated, her gaze becoming secretive, her openness disappearing. Looking away, she said nothing.

Lucy arrived at their table with their drinks and the pie and ice cream. ''How's your mother, Megan? Tell her to come in and visit. I haven't talked to her since y'all came back.''

''Thank you, I will.''

After Lucy left the table, Rick leaned forward. ''You just recently came to town?''

''A month ago.''

Her clipped tones didn't invite conversation.

He frowned. The lady was presenting a puzzle. He assumed she'd been told to approach him by one of the matchmakers. Maybe he was wrong. ''Look, I'm sorry I jumped to conclusions. I figured Mabel or Florence or—'' He stopped as her cheeks flooded with color. Guilt if he ever saw it.

''How did you know?'' she asked with gasp.

He didn't answer at once. The pie and ice cream, already melting, demanded his attention. After he'd digested a tasty bite, he grinned. ''Everyone in town knows those ladies are determined to marry off every single man in the county.'' He shook his head, still grinning. ''Not that I'm accusing you of trying to marry me. They usually start off with a date to one of the barn dances they have around here.''

He thought she'd be even more embarrassed,

maybe even back out of asking him. Too bad. He might have enjoyed dancing with Miss Megan Ford.

Taking another bite, he was enjoying the combination of warm fruit pie and cold ice cream, when she spoke.

"You're wrong, Mr. Astin. We're skipping the date part and going straight to the wedding vows. I'm asking you to marry me."

He sputtered pie and ice cream across the table.

NOT HER MOST shining moment, Megan decided.

She shouldn't have lost her temper, but the man was so sure she was eager to fall at his feet in adoration.

"Don't get your hopes up," she added sharply as he stared at her. "I'm not in admiration of your masculine charms. But I need a husband."

He gave a low chuckle that shivered down her nerves as he wiped off the table. "That's sure a unique approach, Miss Ford."

"I'm serious!" she snapped.

That fascinating left brow slipped up toward his dark hair, but he was still grinning. "Yeah, and I'm the Easter bunny."

Okay, so she hadn't handled it right, but the man didn't have to be sarcastic. She gritted her teeth and waited for him to stop laughing.

"I can offer you five thousand dollars," she said grimly.

The mention of money seemed to sober him up.

She'd thought it would. He didn't have the look of a wealthy man. Mabel Baxter had told her he was trying to operate his ranch on a shoestring, doing most of the work himself.

He put down his fork and leaned forward. "Let me get this straight. You're offering me five thousand dollars to marry you?"

She nodded.

"Why?"

She twisted her hands together. The explanation wasn't as simple as the request. And a lot depended on her convincing the stranger across from her to agree to her proposal. "It's complicated."

"Getting married always is."

His drawl carried a note of bitterness.

"You've been married before?"

He gave a brief nod.

"Do you have children?" That would really make things complicated.

"Nope. I'm not cut out to be a father." He put more pie on his fork. "You're not going to surprise me again, are you?"

The twinkle of humor in his brown eyes was reassuring. When she shook her head no, he even smiled, which made him more handsome.

"Um, the reason I need to marry is to get custody of my niece and nephew." If the man didn't like kids, he probably wouldn't agree. Why hadn't Mabel said anything? She knew why Megan was looking for a husband.

His chewing slowed, as if he was considering her

explanation. After swallowing, he leaned forward. "Where are their parents?"

Her eyes filled with tears. After all, it had only been a few months since she'd lost her sister. "My…my sister's dead."

"And her husband?"

Husband. That word had once meant good things to her. Until Drake Moody had come into her sister's life. "He's in prison."

She could tell her abrupt answer had surprised him, but at least he didn't lose any food. He put his fork down and stared at her. Finally, he said, "Looks to me like you won't have much competition for guardianship."

She pressed her lips tightly together before drawing a deep breath. Then she forced herself to relax. "He'll get out soon. And he'll come after them. Mr. Gibbons said I'd stand a better chance if I'm married."

"Mac? You talked to Mac?"

"Yes, Dr. Gibbons's husband."

"He's good."

"Yes." She knew the man was a good attorney. He'd been honest with her, not offering false promises. That's why she'd made the desperate move of asking this man to marry her.

"Well? What's your answer?" she prodded, staring at him.

RICK BLEW OUT his breath, leaning back against the booth. She wanted an answer now? Automatically, a no rose in his throat. After all, he'd tried marriage once. Who would consider a second marriage? Not him.

"I might be able to come up with another twenty-five hundred," she said, pleading with her blue eyes.

He shook his head, frowning. The money didn't matter. Not that he could tell her that. Someone might discover his secret. Which made his answer hard to explain.

"I've been married once. I don't want to do that again."

"We're not talking about a real marriage. It would be a marriage on paper. We'd stay married until I get the children. Then…then we'll get a divorce."

"Won't the courts be suspicious?" What was he doing, arguing with her?

"We…we might have to wait six months. I could ask Mr. Gibbons."

Damn, he didn't want to tell her no. Those blue eyes tugged at his heart. "Look, we'd have to live together. You don't want to do that."

"We…we can give you your own room. I'll take the children in with me and—"

"Lady, I have to live on the ranch. I have a lot of work to do. I can't live in town." Okay, here was his out. He'd given himself a year to prove himself. He had four months to go.

"Do you have a house?"

"Yeah." He had a big old house, made for families. Too much house for him. He didn't have the time to clean it. He barely kept the kitchen decent. Maybe decent was too nice a word. But he couldn't afford a housekeeper. Not on his present budget. Things had cost more than he'd thought.

"We could move into your house. We'd be quiet. We wouldn't cause you any trouble."

She was desperate, he realized. So desperate she was on the verge of tears. Walking away from Megan Ford would be hard to do. He'd be haunted forever by those big blue eyes.

"What kind of coffee do you make?"

She blinked several times. "What kind? I...I usually grind my own beans. I like—"

"Grind your own beans? Are you serious?"

"Well, yes, but—"

"Tell me you can cook, too."

She gave him a befuddled stare. "Yes, though not as good as my mother."

"Your mother?"

"There's four of us. Me and my mother and the two kids. But two rooms would be enough. I promise we wouldn't take up much space."

"Can you clean house?"

"I don't—why are you asking me these questions?"

"I need a housekeeper and I can't afford to hire one." The idea that had struck him sent a surge of adrenaline through him. He could have a housekeeper and it wouldn't cost him anything. In return, he'd help Megan gain custody of two little kids.

Not a bad trade-off.

"What do you think?" he asked, as she continued to stare at him.

"You're serious?"

"Why not? We'd each get what we needed. A temporary husband for you and a housekeeper for me. Sounds like the perfect bargain." He grinned at her, hoping to chase away those tears that still lingered.

Her eyes narrowed. "I shouldn't have to pay you if I'm going to work for you. Oh! I mean, I already have a job. But Mother and I together could—"

"I agree. No money. Does your mother keep the kids while you're working?" His wife had never worked. Or cleaned house for that matter. He'd had a housekeeper. He wished he still had her. In fact, he'd been having dreams about Maria and her enchiladas, but she'd retired when he left Austin.

"What can you cook?" he asked, his gaze intent on her face.

"You seem to be fixated on food," she muttered, frowning at him.

"If you'd been eating what I have, you would, too."

"You don't have enough money for food?" she asked, her voice rising in horror.

"I have enough money for food, but when I come dragging in at dusk, after putting in twelve or fourteen hours, I don't have the energy to cook anything. Or find a clean pan," he added under his breath, hoping she didn't hear him.

"You don't have any pots and pans?"

"I've got a few." But they were all dirty. He pictured his kitchen as he'd left it this morning. Not a pretty sight.

"We have plenty of kitchen things. We could bring ours and then there'd be enough. We're renting a place month-to-month, so we could move in at the end of the month."

He barely heard her words. All he could think about was sitting down to a decent meal at the end of the day. Coming home to a clean house. Maybe even having his laundry done for him.

Maria had taken care of all that stuff for him. He hadn't even considered those aspects of his life when he left Austin. He'd thought of a breeding bull. Fencing materials. A secondhand tractor. A couple of trucks.

Nothing for the kitchen.

"So, you still haven't told me. What can you cook?"

Chapter Two

"What did he say?" Faith asked, meeting her daughter at the door of their small apartment.

Megan tried to smile. She wanted to reassure her mother. The past year had been hard on her. "He said yes."

Faith closed the door and turned back to Megan. "You don't sound happy about it. Have you changed your mind? You shouldn't marry him if it's not what you want to do, Meggie."

"Megan?" a shrill little voice sounded only seconds before her niece burst into the small living area. "You're here!" Victoria squealed and launched herself into her aunt's arms.

Megan held her close, kissing her little cheek. The child's warmth against her chased away the chill she'd been feeling. She looked over Torie's shoulder. "I'm happy about it, Mom. He's...he's a little strange, but nice," she hurriedly added.

"Where did you go?" Torie demanded, putting her hands on Megan's cheeks and turning her face to her.

"I had to go to a meeting. Were you good for Grandma?"

"Very good. I took my nap, didn't I, Grandma?"

"She did. She just woke up a few minutes ago. Andrew is still sleeping."

The guilty look that covered Victoria's face, plus the cry from another room, told its own story.

"You woke up your brother?" Megan asked Torie.

"I didn't mean to. I thought he would play with me," Torie responded, her eyes filling with tears.

Megan knew she had to be stern with her niece, but not now, not today. She hugged the three-year-old closer. "Then let's go see if he wants to play."

When she and Torie, along with nine-month-old Andrew, returned to the living area, Faith was seated at the breakfast table.

"Let the children play and you come talk to me," Faith ordered.

Megan settled the children with some toys. Andrew sat on the floor, his chubby legs spread wide to give him balance. Torie had several stuffed animals she used to entertain the baby.

Her mother poured her a cup of coffee as she sat at the table. "Why did you say Rick Astin was strange?"

"Because all he wanted to talk about was what we could cook. He wanted to know if you could make enchiladas."

"Didn't you ask him to marry you?" Faith asked, her eyes widening.

"Of course I did. And he agreed. And I don't have to pay him any money," Megan assured her mother, her chin jutting out as she remembered her negotiations.

"Not pay him? Then why is he willing...Megan, he didn't assume...you explained it wouldn't be a real marriage, didn't you?"

"Of course I did. But we'll have to share living quarters if we're going to convince the courts. You knew that."

"Yes, but—we agreed you and I would share the sleeper sofa, the children would have one bedroom, and he could have the other."

"He can't stay here."

Faith's alarm increased, upsetting Megan. The doctor had warned that her mother had to be relieved of stress or it could cause permanent damage to her heart. "Mom, let me explain. Everything's going to work out fine. But he's a rancher. He has to live on the ranch. But he has a big house."

"He does? And we could live with him?"

"Yes. And we're not paying him because we're going to be his housekeepers and cooks during our agreement. So we'll save on rent, too."

"That way we can save more money to pay for the legal bills," Faith said, obviously relieved.

Megan took a deep breath. However much she hated the agreement she'd made, it would be worth it if it brought relief to her mother and saved the kids.

"So we're invited to his house for dinner this

evening, to look at our new living quarters," Megan added, putting on a big smile.

"Tonight?" Faith asked and looked at her watch. "But it's already four o'clock. Let's see, I'll bathe the children. While I'm dressing them, you can have the shower. Then—"

"Mom, he's not going to inspect us. He already agreed."

"But you want to look nice for him, Megan. He should be proud of his new family."

Megan sighed. "I think all he cares about is enchiladas, Mom."

FROM HIS POSITION at the backdoor, Rick took a long, hard look at the kitchen. It was even more of a disaster than he'd remembered. Or wanted to admit.

The sink was piled high with dirty dishes. The cabinets needed cleaning. The trash was overflowing. The long table had a week's worth of mail, empty cereal boxes, more dirty dishes and…uh-oh; a pair of dirty socks.

He looked at his watch. Just after four. He'd invited Megan and her family to dinner at six.

With a sigh, he headed for the phone. The only good meals he'd had since he moved to Cactus were the nights he splurged and ate at The Last Roundup. He'd order a meal to go. If he picked it up at five-thirty, he'd have an hour before then to straighten the kitchen, shower and drive back into town.

Working like a whirlwind, he cleared as much of the kitchen as he could. Just removing all the trash made everything better. But he managed to fill the dishwasher and turn it on before he took a brief shower and threw on a newer pair of jeans and a T-shirt. All his regular shirts were so wrinkled he didn't dare wear them.

He ran for the pickup and zoomed into town. Jamming into a parking spot in front of the restaurant, he vaulted from the vehicle and almost collided with Cal Baxter, the town sheriff.

"Whoa, Rick! You're in a little hurry, aren't you?" Cal asked, clasping Rick's shoulder as he tried to pass him by.

"I've got company coming for dinner," Rick explained. "Your wife's doing the cooking." Cal's wife, Jessica, owned The Last Roundup.

Cal laughed. "Good thinking. Well, slow down on the return trip. I wouldn't want one of my deputies pulling you over."

"Thanks, Cal, I will," he agreed and raced ahead of him into the restaurant.

His luck ran out on the way home. He hit what looked like a piece of cardboard in the road, but it turned out to be metal and ripped his back tire all to pieces.

He muttered a few highly appropriate words, even if they wouldn't be acceptable in polite company, and set to work putting on the spare as fast as he could. The kitchen needed more work, and the rest of the house hadn't even been touched.

By the time he got the tire changed, he needed another shower and it was almost six o'clock. As he reached for the truck door, a four-door sedan passed him. He caught a glimpse of Megan driving.

Damn, the whole agreement was about to go down the drain. All because he was a lousy housekeeper. With a sigh, Rick slid behind the wheel and trailed the sedan to his ranch.

Megan got out of her car and stared at him as he pulled in behind her.

Getting out of the truck, he pasted on a smile. "Hi. I intended to be here to greet you, but I had a flat tire." He couldn't even offer his hand for a greeting. It was smeared with black dirt.

An older woman, a faded version of Megan, got out of the passenger seat. "Hello, I'm Faith Ford. I hope we're not causing you too much trouble."

"No, not at all," he assured her, impressed with his own acting ability. "Uh, I'm not a very good housekeeper, though. I hope you won't be offended by…by everything."

The look on her face reminded him of Maria. She'd always scolded him about his lack of tidiness. But he'd had his mind on other things.

"I explained that you don't have time to clean the house," Megan hurriedly said.

He shot her a grateful look. "Thanks. I have dinner in the truck. Let me get it and we'll go in."

While he gathered the containers of food, Megan and her mother unstrapped the two children from their seats. He was nervous around kids. The few he'd spent time with seemed to constantly scream and complain. These two weren't making any noise. That was a good sign.

He led them to the backdoor. No one used front doors in Cactus. He juggled the containers to pull the door open and stand to one side. The ladies stepped through and he took it as a good sign that they didn't turn around and run out screaming.

He followed them in, discovering them staring around them, a surprised look on their faces.

He must've done a better job than he'd thought. But as he surveyed the kitchen, too, he realized, with a sinking heart, that he'd only made a dent in the mess. He'd cleaned off the table, but he'd done so by making piles on the floor, on the hutch and in one corner of the cabinet. He *had* gotten rid of the socks, but he didn't think it would be good to brag about that.

He'd meant to sweep the floor, but he'd run out of time. The mud he'd tracked in last week after they'd had a spring rain was still there. Dog hair was noticeable. When Daisy barked at the backdoor, he automatically opened the screen for her even as he was trying to figure out what to say.

"Uh, the table's clean," he muttered.

"A doggie!" the little girl squealed, reaching out to Daisy.

"We can't touch the doggie right now, Torie. It's time to eat," Megan said. Then she looked at him, a question in her blue eyes.

"Yeah, I've got the food right here," he assured her, setting the containers on the table.

The two women exchanged a look. Finally, the older one said, "Do you have place mats? Or...or dishes?"

Heck, they could see he had dishes. A lot of them were piled in the sink. He hadn't been able to get them all in the dishwasher.

"There's clean ones in the dishwasher. I'll—"

"I'll get them," Megan said gently. She helped the little girl into one of the chairs at the table. "You sit still, Torie, and do not pet the dog." Then she turned to him and said softly, "You might want to wash up."

He turned bright red. "Uh, yeah, I'll be right back." He hurried to his bathroom and washed. As he looked in the mirror, he realized his white T-shirt had a streak of black on it. Whipping it off, he searched for another shirt.

Much to his disgust, all he could find was a pink one, created when he'd washed it with something red. "Damn, I'm going to look like a sissy. A messy sissy!" he said in disgust. But he had no choice. He couldn't go without a shirt.

The little girl was still seated at the table, but her gaze was on Daisy, who was sitting on her haunches by the door, waiting for Rick.

"If you'll hold Andrew," Megan's mother said as he entered the kitchen, putting her words into action by placing the baby in his arms before he could protest, "I'll help Megan."

He stood there, dumbfounded, while the two women quickly set the table. Then they opened the boxes to set out the food.

"I didn't buy anything for babies," he suddenly realized. "I'm not used to—"

"You don't dislike children, do you, Mr. Astin?" Faith asked, alarm in her voice.

"No, ma'am. That is, I don't dislike them. I haven't been around too many children."

She beamed at him. "You're doing just fine with Andrew."

Surprised, Rick looked down at the little boy he still held clasped to his chest. "Yeah, hey, he's not crying."

MEGAN HID HER GRIN. She didn't want to spoil his sense of accomplishment by telling Rick that Drew seldom cried. Especially when he'd recently been fed.

After getting a look at Rick's home, the kitchen, at least, she decided this cowboy needed to feel good about something. How could anyone live in the middle of disaster? She only hoped he was better at ranching than he was at taking care of himself.

She looked at him out of the corner of her eye. That pink T-shirt was a surprise. It clung to his muscles, showing his strength, but it was an unusual color.

When all the food was on the table, she looked at Rick. "Um, do you—is there any tea, or—"

His face turned brighter than his T-shirt. "I haven't made any."

"We'll drink water," Faith assured him, reaching out to pat his shoulder.

"There are sodas in the fridge," he hurriedly offered.

The little girl immediately asked for a soda, and Rick was relieved that he could please any of them. A hiccup sounded from the baby he was holding and he peered down at him. He seemed content. Two out of four wasn't bad.

Except the two he'd hoped to impress were the two he couldn't count on his side.

Megan took some glasses out of the dishwasher and added ice. Faith had opened the refrigerator and taken out some sodas and put them on the table. Then she turned to him and reached for the baby.

He was amazed at his reluctance to release the little guy. His warmth had been a comfort.

"Does it matter where we sit?" Megan asked.

He shook his head no. But when she joined Torie, he took the seat at that end of the table.

"I like pink," the little girl announced, beaming at him.

Reminded of his unusual attire, he blushed again. "I, um, I'm not very good with laundry."

Megan's mother, sitting on his other side, patted his arm again. "Don't worry about it. I would be a terrible rancher. How long have you lived here?"

The conversation moved a little more smoothly

after that and by the time they'd finished the meal, Rick counted Faith on his side, too.

But Megan hadn't relaxed, hadn't drawn him into conversation, hadn't smiled at him as Faith had. She'd remained silent most of the meal, dealing with the little girl, but not talking to him.

"May we see the rest of the house?" Faith asked as they finished eating.

All of Rick's comfort disappeared. "Um, it's in pretty bad shape, Faith," he said, as he'd been instructed to call her. "I didn't manage to do any work on it today."

"Why don't you just tell us about it, then," Faith said.

Rick smiled at her. The woman was wonderful. He sent a look at Megan, but she ignored him. "Okay. There are five bedrooms. One of them is down here. The rest are upstairs. I could move to the bedroom down here, and let you have the upstairs. There's only one bath up there, though I've been thinking about adding another one."

When he finished his year, he'd made a few plans. But until that year was over, he was sticking to his budget. No matter what.

"Why?"

That single word from Megan drew his attention. "Why what?"

"There's only you. Why would you need another bath upstairs?"

"The bath upstairs is not very large. I'd like a second bathroom added to the master bedroom."

"Megan, I think it's admirable that Rick wants to improve his home," Faith said softly.

There was some kind of rebuke in her words because Megan's cheeks turned red.

Rick rushed into speech. "I can't do anything right now, but I've been thinking about the future. Unfortunately, you all will have to share that small bath if I move downstairs."

"We'll manage," Megan muttered, not looking at him.

"Of course we will. We only have one bath now. Our house in Fort Worth was much larger, but—well, we're glad we're here."

"When do you want to get married?" Rick asked, fearing Megan had changed her mind. She didn't appear as determined tonight as she had earlier in the day.

At her mother's surprised look, he feared he'd blown it. "You did talk to your mother about…I mean—"

"Yes, I know," Faith hurriedly said. "I thought maybe Megan had explained that we need to handle this business right away."

"We didn't get very far in our discussion this afternoon," he confessed.

"That's because all you wanted to talk about was food," Megan said, her chin in the air.

He couldn't hold back a grin. "Now you see why. I'm not much good with domestic details."

Megan rolled her eyes.

Faith was more sympathetic. "It's hard to do everything. I think this arrangement will suit us well."

"Megan mentioned the end of the month," Rick began, relief filling him that he'd hadn't blown the whole thing.

"Must we wait that long?" Faith asked.

"Mother, we've paid rent until then," Megan inserted.

"I know, but that's three weeks away. I don't see any reason to wait."

"You might even get some of your rent back," Rick added, hoping Megan would agree with her mother. Home-cooked meals right away. He smiled.

"You're thinking about food again," Megan accused.

Damn, she was able to read him too easily. He felt a little unnerved.

"Megan, quit teasing Rick. He's being most cooperative."

Megan smothered her groan and dropped her gaze to her half-eaten meal. There was nothing wrong with the food. It had been excellent. But her appetite had dwindled as the evening had progressed.

She had promised to marry the man beside her? To share a house, if not his bed, for at least a year? To see him every day?

Already she was learning to read his thoughts, to feel sympathy for him, to want to help him. She had to remain apart from this man. She wasn't going to fall into the trap that had claimed her sister.

"Today is Saturday. I think Wednesday would be a good day to be married," Faith said, beaming at Rick. "We could move in Thursday, and, by next weekend, be all settled."

"I think that sounds great," he agreed.

He would, Megan thought to herself. He was thinking in terms of his comfort. Selfish man. Suddenly, she was filled with regret. He was providing what she'd asked for. It wasn't his fault she was in the position she was in. She shouldn't hold it against him.

"Okay, fine. Is there a justice of the peace in town who can marry us?"

"Megan, no!" Faith returned, alarm on her face.

"What, Mom?"

"Mr. Brown, the pastor of our church, will marry you." She turned to Rick. "We can't manage a real wedding, but a nice ceremony and then dinner at Jessica's restaurant would make it a festive occasion."

To Megan's fury, Rick smiled at her mother and nodded agreement. "I think you're right. It will make it nice."

"Are you two crazy?" Meg asked, then realized her voice was too shrill and lowered it. "This is a business arrangement, not a romantic occasion."

"But do you want the rest of the town to know that?" Rick asked calmly. "When the time comes for the court to decide who gets the children, do you want them to suspect that it's a business arrangement? Or a romantic, love-at-first-sight marriage?''

Her mother and Rick stared at her, united in their decision, waiting for her response.

First round to them.

Chapter Three

Megan lost a lot of battles in the next few days. Mostly with herself. She might have to pretend that her marriage was a love match, but she wanted to keep her heart whole.

Her sister had fallen for the entire package. Swept off her feet by a wealthy, charming man, she'd felt like Cinderella with her handsome prince. Less than six months after her fairy-tale wedding, Andrea had discovered the flip side of her romance. Prince Charming had grown more and more abusive.

But by then she was already pregnant. She told Megan she had to stay for the sake of Victoria. Then she became pregnant with Andrew. After his birth, Andrea had hoped her marriage would change. It hadn't.

Finally, she'd left Drake. Then he'd asked her to discuss everything with him. He'd picked her up, without her realizing he'd been drinking, and killed her in an automobile accident.

Megan wasn't going to be swayed by romance.

Or hormones.

But it was an uphill battle. Rick Astin was definitely charming. He had a smile that could turn her heart upside down. And he was as handsome as sin.

At least he wasn't wealthy, though he'd offered to foot the bill for the dinner reception at The Last Roundup. She and her mother had argued with him about that. After all, they weren't paying him to marry Megan. They'd finally agreed to split the cost.

With that settled, her mother's attention had turned to Megan's dress. "We'll go into Lubbock to shop."

"No, Mom, we don't have time. I have that cream-colored suit I bought last year."

"But, dear, you should wear white. You'll make a beautiful bride," Faith said, a smile on her face.

Megan was glad her mother was doing better. She'd shown more energy and hope since Saturday night than she had in almost a year. But she was getting carried away.

"If we're going to move to Rick's place on Thursday, we need to do some cleaning out there," she pointed out, knowing her mother would be distracted with their move. "You know he's a terrible housekeeper."

"Yes, the poor dear. He needs someone to make a home for him. Cal says he's a hard worker. Everyone likes him."

Megan ground her teeth. According to her

mother, Rick was perfection. But then she'd thought the same thing about Drake at first, too.

"We've set everything up with Reverend Brown. We've made reservations with Jessica. I have something to wear. Let's go to Rick's and see what we can do to get the house ready," Megan suggested.

She'd been right. Her mother fell for her distraction. "Yes. If we go now, we can put the kids down for a nap, giving us some uninterrupted time."

"Actually, Florence's housekeeper volunteered to keep the kids for the day," Megan told her. Florence Greenfield, wife of one of the doctors, was an old friend of Faith's, one of the ladies who had suggested Rick as a potential husband.

"How wonderful. I'll call and see if we can drop them off right now."

In the end, Megan found herself one in a small army of women. Her mother's friends, Florence, Mabel Baxter, Ruth Langford and Edith Hauk joined them, as well as several of their housekeepers.

The old house began to come alive as lemon-fresh scent replaced dust, changing Rick's disaster to a comfortable home. Folding a white T-shirt reminded Megan of Rick's pink shirt Saturday night, and his embarrassment. It brought a smile to her face.

"You look happy," Mabel said, catching her by surprise.

"Um, yes, of course," she agreed, remembering the role she had agreed to play.

"I'm glad everything is working out. Now, we need to move Rick's belongings downstairs. Why don't you come direct the change?"

Megan swallowed. She didn't want to make decisions for Rick. But she had no choice.

When it got late in the afternoon, the crew of women began to disperse. After all, they had their own homes and families to deal with. Megan wanted to hang the freshly washed curtains for Torie's room before she left, and Mabel offered to take Faith to get the children and take them to their apartment.

"I should be finished in a few minutes, Mom, if you want to wait."

"No, dear, I'm tired. I think I'd better go on with Mabel."

"Okay," Megan agreed, frowning. She hoped her mother hadn't overdone it today.

As Mabel and her mother were leaving, Mabel said, "There's a casserole in the oven. It needs to come out in half an hour." Then she disappeared out the door.

Megan realized some of the women had brought in bags of groceries, but she hadn't realized they'd cooked. She moved to the oven and opened it. A wonderful aroma filled the room.

With a grin, she realized Rick was going to be pleased. It was some kind of enchilada casserole. She checked to be sure the timer was set and closed the oven. She needed to finish her chore and get out of there.

Then she realized she couldn't leave until Rick returned or the casserole would be ruined.

With a grimace, she went upstairs to hang the curtains. Surely he'd come in soon. It was almost six o'clock.

An hour and a half later, Megan was pacing the floor. It was almost dark. When was the man going to appear? What was he doing?

She'd called her mother to explain why she hadn't arrived, but her mother hadn't been surprised.

"Most ranchers work until the light goes, dear. He'll be there soon. Why don't you share his supper and then come home?"

"No, I'll be home as soon as he shows up."

"But we've already eaten—"

"I can take care of myself, Mom. I'll see you in a little while."

RICK HAD INTENDED to cut his day a little shorter because he'd promised himself he'd give some time to cleaning the house tonight. Faith had asked if she and Megan could come out today to start moving in and he'd reluctantly agreed, telling her the house would be unlocked.

He should've cleaned on Sunday, but even Sundays sometimes required work. It was calving season. And today had been particularly busy. He was filthy and tired.

Next week, after his marriage, he would come

home to a clean house and a hot meal. That idea brought a smile to his weary lips.

He parked his pickup near the backdoor and struggled out, ready to drag himself up the steps. He came to an abrupt halt, however, when he discovered a frowning Megan standing at the backdoor.

"Something wrong?" he asked, speeding up his walk.

"Where have you been?" she asked, instead of answering his question.

"Delivering calves."

"You mean you were actually working?"

Her utter surprise irritated him. "Naw, I was sunbathing by the pond in the back pasture." He regretted his sarcasm as her cheeks flushed. "Why are you still here? Is there a problem?"

"No. I waited to take the casserole out when it finished cooking. Then, I thought it would be rude to leave, so I waited, thinking you'd be here any minute."

He picked out the key word. "Casserole? You fixed dinner?"

"Not me. One of the ladies who helped us today."

"Well, let's eat. I'm starving."

He started to move past her and saw her nose wrinkle in distaste. "Uh, I'll grab a quick shower first," he promised even as his stomach protested the wait.

She followed him into the house. "You go ahead. I'll set out the food and then leave."

"You're not staying to eat?"

"No. I need to go to the apartment and help Mom put the kids to bed." She didn't meet his gaze, which made him wonder if she was lying, but he was too hungry to care.

"Okay."

He was halfway across the kitchen when his surroundings pierced his fog of hunger and weariness. The room gleamed in the fading light and smelled great. "What happened?"

"To what?"

"The kitchen. Man, you must've worked all day to get it to look like this. Nice job, Megan." He turned to smile at her, but she was still frowning.

"We had a lot of help. Mom's friends, the ones who recommended you, came to help."

"Ah, the matchmakers."

"The matchmakers?"

"That's what everyone calls them now, since they had a contest to marry off their sons. You know, Mac, Tuck, Spence and Cal."

"They were just being helpful to me," she muttered and turned her back on him. "Hurry and clean up before your dinner gets too cold."

"Yes, ma'am," he said and bounded up the stairs, spurred on by his hunger.

The hot shower refreshed him, even though it was a quick one. He stepped out and grabbed a towel, doing a quick rubdown. Then, wrapping the towel around his waist, even though Megan was supposed to be gone, he hurried into his bedroom for clean jeans and T-shirt.

And found nothing.

His bedroom was spotless. And the chest of drawers was empty. He opened the closet. Empty. Obviously, the ladies today had taken over the entire house. Now that he thought about it, the bath was immaculate, too. Or it was until he'd showered.

Maybe they moved his things to the downstairs bedroom. He came down the stairs, reaching the bottom as the kitchen door swung open. Megan ran smack into him, her hands coming to rest on his bare chest.

"Oh!"

"Megan! I thought you were leaving."

She backed away and he grabbed for his towel, afraid his modesty was about to disappear.

MEGAN TRIED TO look anywhere but at him, but her gaze kept returning to that magnificent expanse of chest. The muscles were big and brawny and coated with dark hair that tapered down to the white terry cloth towel.

"Are…are you eating without any clothes on?"

"No! At least, I hadn't planned on it. But all my things are missing from the bedroom."

"Sorry, I should've told you. We moved you to the downstairs bedroom. You said—"

"That's fine. I just hadn't realized the extent of your efforts. The house looks great, by the way."

She couldn't look him in the eye. She was acting like a teenage girl who'd never seen a man's body before. She was a nurse, for heaven's sake. "You'd better get dressed."

"Okay. Did you decide to stay and eat with me?"

"No, my car won't start. I wondered if you could look at it." She hated asking, but she'd called the one mechanic in town, and he couldn't come out until morning. Her mother had the children already in bed, and Megan had decided the only practical thing to do was ask Rick for help.

"Before I eat?" he asked, his voice filled with despair.

"No. No, I'll eat with you, if you don't mind. Could you look at it after?"

"Sure. Be glad to. Now that I don't have to do any cleaning tonight, I have lots of time," he agreed, giving her a smile that sped up her breathing.

"Okay," she agreed, turning her back on him. "Dinner will be ready when you're dressed." She had to get away from the near naked man before she reached out to touch that warm flesh again.

He reappeared only a couple of minutes later, taking a deep breath as he came through the door. "That smells like enchiladas."

"One of the ladies made it after I mentioned you liked enchiladas. It's some kind of enchilada casserole."

Megan was surprised when Rick held her chair

for her. She hurriedly slid into the seat, then he took the chair across from her.

He offered no conversation until after he'd eaten at least half of his helping of the casserole. Megan remained silent also. He'd put in more than a twelve-hour day and she knew he must be exhausted.

So when he finally spoke, it shocked her. "This is great. Great food, and the house looks wonderful. You must've worked hard today."

She smiled her thanks. "Not as hard as you. If delivering calves is anything like babies, you must be very tired."

"There were a couple of hard deliveries. Have you ever pulled a calf?"

"No. And I think I'm glad. That doesn't sound pleasant."

He grinned. "Maybe not, but a healthy newborn is worth the effort. The crop today looks good."

"Congratulations, then." She remembered something she wanted to ask him. "When we cleaned and everything, I noticed all the computer equipment in your bedroom downstairs. Are you sure you'll have enough room?"

"Yeah." He continued eating, apparently unconcerned.

"Mother and I can share a room, leaving you the master bedroom."

He stopped eating and frowned at her. "That's not necessary. I want you to be comfortable. If today's any example, you and your mother are going to make me a lot more comfortable.''

"We'll try."

"Think you could get this recipe?"

She rolled her eyes. The man thought with his stomach. Her gaze dropped to that flat, muscular area of his body. When she lifted her gaze again, it slammed into his. "Uh, probably."

"Good."

She struggled for another topic of conversation. "Uh, you must like computers."

His fork stopped halfway to his mouth.

Megan raised an eyebrow when he glared at her before taking a bite. "Is something wrong?"

"No. I like computers, okay?"

His aggressive attitude bothered her. "I didn't mean to intrude. But you've got a lot of expensive equipment in that room. Maybe you shouldn't leave the door unlocked."

"No one locks up out here in the country."

"Oh. Do you…do you spend a lot of time on the computer?"

He put his fork down. "Not now. In the winter, I do a little—that is, I work at the computer. I'm developing a system that helps me keep track of things here on the ranch."

Relief flooded Megan, surprising her. She hadn't realized how worried she'd been. After all, she was going to marry the man. "Oh, good. That could be helpful to a lot of people."

"Yeah," he assured her with a grin. "But I don't

have time for much right now. Not with calves being born day and night.''

''At night? Are you going back out again tonight?''

He rubbed the back of his neck, then shrugged his shoulders. ''I brought a couple of cows in for the night. I'll check on them later.''

''What about the vet?''

His brown eyes looked puzzled. ''What about him? Are you interested in him?''

''No!'' Megan returned, her cheeks flushing. ''I meant did you call the vet to help with the calves.''

''You don't know much about ranching, do you?''

''No, I'm from the city,'' she said defensively, stiffening her shoulders. ''And it doesn't matter. After all, I'm not really going to be a rancher's wife. It's just pretend.''

He looked away. ''Yeah, pretend.''

Megan stared at him in alarm. ''You still want to do this, don't you?''

RICK STARED at the beautiful woman across from him. She really needed to rethink her question. *This* could mean a lot of different things, including some highly stimulating—he halted his thoughts before he got carried away.

Clearing his throat, he nodded. ''Yeah.''

''There's also chocolate cake, if you've finished the casserole,'' she said, watching him.

He couldn't help the pleasure that filled him. "Homemade chocolate cake?"

"Yes. Mom made it."

"I'd love some."

She got up from the table and moved to the counter. He hadn't noticed the cake plate sitting there, but he practically drooled when she removed the cover. He loved chocolate cake.

After putting a piece in front of him, she began clearing the table.

"Hey, I'll do that," he protested.

"No need. I'm not going to have cake, and you've agreed to look at my car for me. It's a fair exchange. In fact, I'll probably be in your debt if you can fix my car."

"So we're going to work on the barter system? You do something for me and I do something for you?"

She looked embarrassed, which only made her skin more tantalizing. He wanted to warm his fingers on her cheeks.

"This isn't a normal marriage. I think we need to establish some rules."

"Okay. What is a chocolate cake worth? 'Cause I'm going to be needing a lot of it."

"You like it? I'll tell Mom."

"Like it? I think your mother is a genius. This is the best chocolate cake I've ever had." He added his best smile with the compliment.

Megan chuckled and he loved the sound. It was husky, warm, inviting. It made him want to hold her against him, feel the laughter move through her body.

Whoa! He was going to be in big trouble if he thought that way.

"You're too easy. Mom will love cooking for you."

"Good."

They stared at each other, tension building. Finally, she moved back to the sink, grabbing the dishcloth as if it were a life raft. "I'll...I'll finish cleaning while you look at my car."

"Okay. I'd better wash my hands first. Wouldn't want to get chocolate icing on your car." He moved to the sink and she hurriedly backed away. "I don't bite," he said, keeping his voice mild.

"No, of course not. I didn't want to get in your way."

Rick didn't believe her. He'd felt the tension a moment ago. The same tension they'd felt when they'd run into each other in the hall. When he was naked. And wished she was.

Was he crazy to think he could share the house with this woman and not feel anything? He couldn't find relief somewhere else, not if he was married to her. He was about to enter a celibate period in his life.

About to? He almost snorted with derisive laughter. He'd been celibate for a couple of years now. After his divorce, he'd tried dating, but he discovered the women he'd met had a hidden agenda. First him, then his money. Whatever it took.

So he'd accepted a different life-style. And been happy with it until today. Or actually Saturday when he'd first met Megan Ford. What was it about her that stirred him?

Other than her beauty. Her body. Her smile. Her sad story. Her selflessness. Her family.

He shook his head. He could go on listing things he liked about her forever.

"You won't look at my car?"

"What? Of course, I will. I said I would."

"But you were shaking your head no."

He smiled at her, barely restraining the urge to drop a kiss on her soft lips. "I was thinking about something else. I'll go look at your car right now."

"Thank you," she said, offering him that special smile again.

He almost stumbled in his hurry to move away before he forgot why he should.

"I'll be outside."

She nodded.

He turned his back and rushed outside, taking a deep breath of the spring night air.

Then he moved to the economy sedan she drove. Like he was a mechanic. Well, he could at least look at it. He knew a little about cars.

She'd left the keys in the ignition. He slipped behind the wheel and turned them, just in case she'd been wrong. No such luck.

He reached down and released the hood and got out of the car. With the porch light on, he thought he'd be able to see well enough to tell if the damage was something he could handle.

Propping up the hood, he scanned the motor. Then his gaze reached the battery.

Bingo.

The negative battery wire was disconnected. He frowned. Why would that happen? Driving on a rough road wouldn't pull the wire loose. It probably required a wrench to loosen it.

Which meant the damage was deliberate.

A sinking feeling settled in his stomach.

It looked like the matchmakers were at work again.

Chapter Four

Megan watched Rick from the kitchen window. The dishes were all rinsed and put in the dishwasher, but she hadn't started it. It only had a few things in it.

What was she supposed to do now? Rick was bent over her motor, like he knew what was wrong. She could offer to help, but she knew almost nothing about cars. She'd been raised in a female household since her father had died when she was a little girl.

Maybe she should see if Rick had left his dirty clothes upstairs. She could put them in the washer. Running up the stairs, she found the clothes he'd been wearing when he came in just where she'd expected to find them. In a pile on the floor of the bathroom.

Men! But maybe picking up his clothes was worth it if he fixed her car. She went to the downstairs bedroom to collect the towel he'd used.

She sighed as she looked around the room. He was really going to be crowded in here, with all the computer equipment. He had several computers, a fax machine, two printers, and some other things she couldn't identify. It did seem excessive for a rancher.

If all this equipment was in his master bedroom, he'd have more room. It was the largest bedroom in the house. Her mother had insisted she take the master bedroom, even though she'd protested. Maybe she should offer to trade with Rick. He could—

"Megan?"

She returned to the kitchen, clutching her armful of dirty clothes. "Yes? Did you fix it?"

"Yeah, I did." Then he frowned. "What are you doing with those smelly clothes?"

"I thought I'd put them in the washer."

"I can pick up after myself."

His voice was hard, unfriendly, which puzzled her.

"I'm just trying to keep the house clean. Remember, that was our agreement."

"I didn't mean for you to pick up after me constantly. I can take care of that." His face turned red. "I know it didn't look like it the other night, but—"

"Rick, it's okay. You fixed my car. I'm grateful. I wash your clothes, you're grateful. Okay?"

"You make things sound simple."

Some of the tension had left his voice and Megan breathed a sigh of relief. "I think it is. Even if you hadn't fixed my car, you're doing a wonderful thing for us.''

"Uh, about the car. I fixed it."

She beamed at him. "Yes, I can't thank you enough. It would've been expensive to have the mechanic come out in the morning."

"Uh, yeah. Did you tell your mother the car wouldn't start?"

"No, I haven't said anything yet. Why? Shouldn't I tell her?" There had been something in his voice that told her everything wasn't right.

"Well, I'm not sure, but I think someone sabotaged your car."

"Someone what? You think someone actually broke my car on purpose? That's ridiculous, Rick. The only people here today were the ladies and me and Mom."

"I know, Megan, but—"

"Why, even if they wanted to, and I can't think of a single reason they would, they're women. They wouldn't know how to do anything to the car."

Rick laughed. "You have a lot to learn."

She stiffened. "Why are you laughing?"

"Because the only one of those ladies who hasn't lived on a ranch most of her life is Florence. And I suspect she could manage as well as any of them. Mabel, Edith and Ruth could probably take a tractor apart and rebuild it before you could blink an eye."

"Why?"

"Why? Because a rancher's wife is his partner, his helpmate, his—his wife."

Megan waved away his words. "No, I mean why would they want to mess up my car? They're our friends."

"Ask their sons."

His cryptic words didn't make any sense to Megan. She stared at him. "What are you talking about?"

Rick rubbed the back of his neck again, a movement Megan was beginning to realize meant he wasn't sure what to say. When he did speak, it wasn't to explain his words.

"You'd better go put those clothes in the washing machine before you need a bath yourself."

She hadn't even realized she still held the stinky clothes. With a huff of frustration, she charged down the hall to the utility room and dumped the clothes into the washing machine. Quickly adding soap, she twirled the dial and started the washer. Then she returned to the kitchen.

"Well? Are you ready to explain?"

"Is there any coffee?"

With another frustrated sigh, she prepared his percolator and plugged it in.

"We can talk while it's perking," she suggested, waving him to the table.

He didn't look happy, but he accepted her invitation, settling himself in the same seat he'd used when he ate dinner. "Look, Megan, you're going to think I'm crazy, but I think the ladies were matchmaking."

She did think he was crazy. Obviously, he hadn't

thought things through. With a patient smile, she said, "You're wrong, Rick. They have no need to matchmake. We're getting married, remember? They were kind enough to suggest you when we explained our problem. But we've come to an agreement, so there's no difficulty."

He rubbed the back of his neck again.

Which was beginning to drive her crazy. "Well? I'm right, aren't I?"

After a minute, he said, "Sure. Yeah, sure. Um, do you want me to follow you back into Cactus? To make sure you get home all right?"

"No. You're just saying that, aren't you? You don't think I'm right." She leaned forward, determination in every bone. "Explain, please."

He looked like a cornered bear, big, powerful and irritated. "I agreed with you."

"But you didn't mean it."

"How do you know? We just met Saturday. You don't know me that well."

Strangely enough, she wondered if his words were true. She thought she was beginning to know him, to feel comfortable with him. At least most of the time. Not when he was naked, of course, but that wasn't even a consideration. Just an accident.

"Maybe I know you better than you think."

"I don't think so."

"So," she said, drawing the word out slowly, "I should believe you're upset that I thought logically and you didn't?"

The immediate spark of irritation in his eyes

brought a smile to her lips. Yes, she was getting to know him.

"What are you smiling about?"

Her smile widened. "I'm trying to be a pleasant companion, Rick. Hadn't you rather I smile than be an old sourpuss?"

He ignored her teasing. Leaning forward, he covered her clasped hands, resting on the table in front of her, with his. Immediately, her hands were surrounded with warm flesh, reminding her of when she'd fallen against him in the hallway.

"It's not a question of logic. These ladies are romantics," he explained.

"So they should be happy. We're getting married." She was beginning to get an inkling of what he was trying to explain and she wanted to deny it.

"We're cementing a business agreement."

Her chin rose and her smile disappeared. "So?"

"So, they want romance."

"But surely they wouldn't—why, it would be wrong to break my car. Against the law." She frowned more deeply. "I'm sure they wouldn't do that."

"Cal's mother put holes in condoms when she was trying to get Cal married."

Megan's eyes widened in horror and she gasped, "No!"

"It's true."

"How do you know? Cal wouldn't tell anyone that. Why, he and Jessica have the prettiest little boy. He wouldn't—"

"We were sitting in The Last Roundup around Christmastime. The ladies were scheming against some guy named Joe Chamblee. I said I didn't think there was much they could do to get someone married if they didn't want to marry. Cal told me what his mother had done as a warning."

Megan was floored. To think that his mother would do something like that to Cal. Her own son. Messing up Megan's car, in a way that was easily fixed, didn't seem nearly as bad.

"But why?" As he opened his mouth, Megan interrupted. "I know you said for romance, but why would my having car trouble do anything?"

Both their gazes immediately flew to the clasped hands in the middle of the table. Then they both jerked away, as if by touching they were endangering themselves.

"Look, if I'm right, they may try other things," Rick said, his voice rough. "I want to be honest with you. I'm not interested in any *real* marriage. I don't believe in it anymore. And nothing they can do will induce me to submit myself to that kind of misery again."

Megan hurried to reassure him even as she felt a twinge in her chest at the desolation on his face. "Me, neither. After all, marriage killed my sister. I have no intention of marrying. For real, I mean."

Rick stood, towering over her. "I hope you don't mean that, Megan. Eventually, I hope you meet your Mr. Wonderful. But…but, for now, at least we understand each other. We're not going to be caught in their trap. Right?''

''Right.'' She started to extend her hand for a handshake to seal their agreement. Then she remembered it would be better not to touch again. So she rose and stared at the handsome man across the table from her.

''I guess I'd better go. May we start moving in our things tomorrow?''

''Yeah, sure. I'd like to offer to help, but—''

''You have calves to deliver. It's okay. We'll be fine.'' She turned to go and he followed her to the kitchen door.

''You sure you don't want me to follow you?''

''No, that's not necessary. I'll be fine.''

''So I'll see you tomorrow?''

She turned to look at him. It had sounded like it mattered to him if she saw him. But no, that couldn't be true.

''Maybe. But there's plenty of casserole left for your dinner tomorrow. And lots of chocolate cake.''

''Yeah. If I'm not careful, I'll get too fat to get on a horse,'' he said with a grin, patting his flat stomach.

Megan laughed, but her gaze concentrated on his lean frame, his hard muscles. ''I doubt it.''

''Good night, then. Thanks for all you've done.''

''You, too,'' she said, lifting her gaze to mingle with his warm brown one. She gave a hurried wave and ran to her car.

It was time to get the hell out of Dodge.

RICK SPENT the night in the downstairs bedroom. The bed wasn't as comfortable as his. Not because the mattress was old, but because it was a standard-size mattress, not king-size like his bed.

But it was a pleasure to rise to a clean house, freshly laundered clothes. He even had a piece of chocolate cake after he'd eaten his cereal. No one was there to tell him not to.

He decided he'd better enjoy it. Once the women invaded his territory, he figured they'd preach about nutrition.

He lingered over a second cup of coffee. He needed to get to the barn and check on the cows he'd brought in the night before. And then cover the pastures. Jose was supposed to work with him today. An extra pair of eyes and hands.

The sound of a car had him leaping to his feet and crossing to the kitchen window. When he realized what he was doing, he dumped the rest of his coffee into the sink and stalked out of the kitchen.

He'd been sitting there hoping Megan would come before he left the house.

He never paid attention to cars on the road. But this morning he'd immediately noticed. And hurried to see if it turned into his place.

He'd better be careful, or those interfering ladies were going to cause him a hell of a lot of trouble. He hurried out to the barn, ready to turn his attention to his cows.

MEGAN WORKED with Dr. Gibbons, or Samantha, as she'd suggested Megan call her. Megan had never worked for a doctor who treated her nurse like a human being. It was an interesting and pleasant phenomenon. Since Samantha had a daughter almost twenty months old and was expecting another baby in October, she only worked part-time. Megan's hours were the same.

Samantha greeted her as she reached the office Tuesday morning. "How are you settling in?"

"Fine. We've been here a month, you know."

"Oh, I know. But I meant at Rick's place."

Megan's cheeks flushed. "You heard?"

"I heard that there was a massive cleaning. Florence mentioned several times at dinner last night that men were hopeless when it came to housework."

The two ladies grinned at each other.

"I'm not sure that's true," Megan said, "but with Rick's long hours on the ranch, he doesn't have much time for housework."

"I guess not. It is calving season. Mac's planning on taking off a couple of weeks when his friends do roundup."

"But he's a lawyer," Megan protested.

"A man never stops being a cowboy. He loves it. Every year he helps them."

"Rick could use some help. He only has one hand who comes a couple of days a week."

"I'll ask Mac if Rick can be included. But he'll have to help the others."

"Of course. That would be great," Megan said with a smile, hoping Rick would be pleased. She loved to see that slow grin that warmed her to her toes.

No! No, that wasn't the reason. She was just trying to fulfill her role. A rancher's wife. Even if it was only a pretense.

"Are we ready?" Samantha asked.

Megan blinked several times, pulling herself back to the present. "Yes, of course. The first patient is Mr. Herkimer Jones. He's complaining of a painful knee."

Samantha sighed. "That's the problem with a small town. Everyone knows everyone else's problems. Herk has arthritis, but he won't accept it."

"Poor man. Can you help him?"

"We're trying some new things, but he won't always follow directions. Show him in."

DR. GIBBONS finished her office hours at one on Tuesdays and Thursdays. After tidying the examination rooms, Megan finished the notes on the patients they'd seen, then stopped by Samantha's office.

"I've finished. Is there anything else I need to do?"

"No, thanks, Megan. I appreciate your work. It was too much for Doc's nurse before you got here."

Megan smiled, appreciating the compliment. "I'm enjoying it."

"Good. See you tomorrow afternoon."

They alternated their Tuesday-Thursday schedule by working afternoons on Monday and Wednesday. Then they worked on Saturday mornings every other week. It left Megan more time to spend with the children and her mother.

She hurried to the apartment they'd rented in town. Her mother had a sandwich ready for her.

"You sit down and eat. Then we're ready to go. Torie and I packed while Drew took his morning nap," Faith informed her.

"I put my toys in a big sack," Torie said proudly.

Megan loved the happiness in her little face. When Andrea had left Drake and moved back home, Torie had been a silent, unhappy child. Not because she missed her father, but because her mother was unhappy.

"What a good helper you are," Megan bragged, giving her a hug.

Torie beamed back. "Now we can go play with Daisy."

"I don't know if Daisy will be at the house. I think she works with Rick."

"A dog has to work? What does she do?" Torie asked, her blue eyes, like Megan's, rounding in wonder.

"She makes the cows go where Rick wants them to go... I think." Megan looked at her mother for confirmation.

"You're probably right. We've got a lot to learn, don't we?" Faith said cheerfully.

Megan frowned. Her mother somehow made their arrangement sound permanent. Or maybe she, Megan, was hypersensitive. She sighed and ate her lunch. It didn't matter. They had to go through with the marriage anyway.

"Did you talk to Dr. Gibbons about not working tomorrow?"

Megan looked at her mother. "Why would I do that?"

"Because tomorrow is your wedding day, of course!" Faith exclaimed. "In fact, I think you should take off the rest of the week."

"Mother, I can't do that. Besides, the wedding isn't until seven tomorrow night. I'll be through work long before that."

"And Thursday morning? I suppose you're going into work like it was any other day?" Faith sounded offended at the idea.

"Mom, we may have to pretend this is a…a romantic marriage, but you and I know the truth."

"Rick—"

"As long as you fix him breakfast, Rick won't complain about anything."

"Well, of course, I'll fix him breakfast. That dear boy is half-starved to death. But I think—"

"Time to go," Megan announced, rising from the table, her sandwich half-eaten. But she couldn't listen to her mother's opinion about her marriage any longer. Her words, immediately heard by Torie, stopped her mother's argument.

"Daisy! Daisy!" the child shrieked at the top of her voice.

"I had no idea she was that interested in dogs," Faith muttered.

"I'm going to pack a few things, then I'll be ready," Megan said, heading for the bedroom she shared with her mother. One of the benefits of their move would be a room to herself. She loved her mother and the children, but she needed some privacy occasionally.

THEY UNPACKED THE children's belongings first. The bed in Torie's room was full-size, and the little girl rolled all over it.

"I get the whole bed, Aunt Megan? No one else will sleep with me?"

"That's right, Torie. You're a big girl now, and you can have your own room."

"I can have tea parties, and everything!"

"Yes, you can, baby. Maybe soon we can find a small table for you."

"Megan?" Faith called. She'd gone to the kitchen and Megan could hear her coming up the stairs.

"Yes, Mom?"

Her mother appeared in the doorway. "I've been looking at the bedroom downstairs."

"Rick's? You shouldn't have—"

"I think I should take that room. Then he can

move all his computer equipment to the master bedroom where there's more room.''

''But—''

''He's going to be much too crowded downstairs. And the king-size bed will fit him better. Unless you object to giving it up?''

''No, I don't object, but I think we should wait until Rick gets here to make a decision.''

''I'm going to move his clothes back upstairs and settle in. The boy is so generous, he'd probably refuse to change. But this is for the best.'' With a wave of her hand, Faith sailed out the door, full steam ahead.

Actually, Megan agreed with her mother. She'd thought the same thing. And it seemed only fair, with all Rick was doing for them, that he be comfortable. So she didn't protest her mother's decision. She, Megan, needed to be upstairs to take care of Drew if he awoke during the night. Or occasionally Torie had bad dreams.

She didn't want her mother having to get up to tend to the children. She needed her rest.

So, the decision was a good one. She continued unpacking for Torie, her mind on other things than her husband-to-be.

Until it occurred to her that there was only one bathroom upstairs. She was going to have to share a bathroom with Rick Astin, who looked great in a bath towel.

Chapter Five

When Rick pulled up beside the house that evening around seven, he knew Megan and her family were there. The car, of course, told him someone was there, but there were lights on all over the house.

As he stepped into the kitchen, he sensed movement and liveliness that chased away the normal loneliness he felt when he came home. Daisy, beside him, raised her nose and sniffed, as if she too could tell a difference.

"Oh! You're back," Faith exclaimed as she stepped into the kitchen, beaming at him. "You go clean up. I'll have your dinner on the table in five minutes. I made Megan wait to eat with you, even though the children and I ate earlier. Shoo, now! You don't want it to get cold."

Rick smiled and stepped past his future mother-in-law. Good thing he agreed with her plans, because he didn't think she'd be easy to derail. He automatically turned to the stairs before remembering that he'd been moved. Changing directions, he went to the downstairs bathroom and stripped out of his dirty clothes.

He felt years younger when he stepped out of the hot shower. Wrapping the towel around his waist, he opened the door to go to his new bedroom. Once there, he pulled open a drawer for clean underwear and found his choices to be silky and lacy.

He frowned, surveying the drawer. Not his underwear. Surely Megan hadn't decided to cohabit without telling him? Somehow he didn't think so. Especially when he couldn't find any of *his* clothes.

Were they going to hide his belongings each day? Did he have to have a treasure hunt to find his underwear?

He strode back into the hall, a frown on his face, as he heard Faith calling Megan to come to dinner.

"Is Rick here?" Megan called back down the stairs.

"Yes, I am, and where's my underwear?" he roared back. He was getting damned uncomfortable running around in a towel.

Faith opened the door to the kitchen and Megan appeared at the top of the stairs.

"Oh, dear, I forgot to tell you I changed bedrooms with you," Faith said, smiling an apology.

Megan bit her bottom lip and stepped aside, silently inviting him to climb the stairs.

With a rueful smile in Faith's direction, he ascended the stairs. When he reached the top, Megan was standing so close he could smell the fresh flower scent she always seemed to wear.

"I'm sorry. I meant to catch you before you showered," Megan said.

"At least it's not winter," he muttered, figuring he'd catch pneumonia if he wandered around in a towel when it was freezing outside. "I'll be down in a minute for dinner."

After dressing, he hurried to the kitchen to find Megan seated at the table and Faith nowhere in sight.

"Where's your mom?"

"She's upstairs with the kids. She insisted I wait and eat with you. I hope you don't mind."

"Not at all. Where's the enchilada casserole?" The table held several bowls of vegetables and a covered dish.

"Mom didn't think you should eat leftovers, so she cooked a roast."

His eyes lit up as his stomach rumbled.

"Don't tell me you like roast better than enchiladas," she teased, relaxing with a smile for the first time.

He grinned. "I'm a Texan. We never turn down beef."

He slid into the chair across from her, thinking how nice it was to have company at a meal. How nice it was to have company, period. Living with the four Fords would take away that loneliness that had bothered him for the past eight months.

Of course, when they left, he'd be lonelier than ever.

Not a happy thought.

Megan passed him a bowl of creamed potatoes. Then she removed the lid to the covered dish, revealing thick slices of roast beef. He inhaled the aroma with satisfaction.

"I'm going to be spoiled pretty soon," he muttered as he served himself.

"Because you have dinner cooked for you?" Megan asked.

"Oh, yeah." He took a bite of the roast beef and slowly chewed. Then he sighed. "Definitely."

"I don't think having dinner cooked for you is too much spoiling. Most men have that privilege." Megan served herself a small amount of food.

"Is that all you're going to eat?" he asked, frowning.

She looked up, surprised. "Why, yes. I haven't worked as hard as you."

"Did you work at the doctors' office today?"

"Yes," she said, going on to explain her work schedule.

"You don't want to work full-time?"

"No. I don't want to put too much of a burden on my mother. Her health hasn't been good lately."

Rick continued to ask questions about Megan's life. Somehow, he needed to know more about this woman. The conversation made the meal even more enjoyable.

They'd almost finished when the little blond girl burst into the kitchen, wearing a pink nightgown. "I finished my bath, Megan." Torie ran to her, throwing her arms around her aunt's waist.

Rick stared at the child. "Are all of you spending the night?"

"No!" Megan returned, her cheeks red. "But Mother decided to bathe the children here. When they ride in the car, they go to sleep. This way we can tuck them into bed without waking them."

"Oh. You should've gone home earlier instead of waiting on me." He felt guilty about keeping the kids from their beds.

Megan stiffened in her chair. "We thought you would enjoy a hot meal."

"Hey, I did! I wasn't complaining," he hurriedly explained. "I was thinking of the kids."

"I like it here," Torie insisted, smiling at him.

Rick couldn't hold back a smile in return. The child looked like his idea of an angel. "I'm glad."

"Don't get puffed up about it," Megan told him. "She likes it here because of Daisy."

The dog, now lying in a corner in the kitchen, raised her head at hearing her name. Rick turned to soothe his faithful companion.

"Can Daisy play?" Torie whispered.

"After you've had your bath?" Rick wasn't sure of the rules, but he thought Megan wouldn't approve.

"No, Torie. You'd get all dirty again," Megan said, her voice soft with love.

A fierce yearning surprised Rick. He hadn't heard anyone speak to him with such warmth since his mother died.

But it was a momentary weakness. Nothing

more. He certainly didn't want the woman across from him to feel anything for him.

MEGAN WAS GRATEFUL for Torie's interruption. There had been an intimacy developing between her and Rick that worried her. The man across from her was too easy to talk to.

"But Daisy's not dirty," Torie insisted, standing on tiptoes to see the dog.

"I think she might need a bath," Rick said, his brown eyes solemn. "She rolled in the dirt."

"When does she get her bath? She could share with me," Torie offered. She edged closer to Rick. Megan had noticed that she had kept her distance from the man so far.

Rick smiled at the child. "Sweetheart, I don't think that would be a good idea. Daisy usually bathes in the creek."

Torie took another step closer and Megan held her breath, hoping Rick didn't scare the child.

"Can I bathe in the creek?"

Rick appeared to seriously consider her question. "Hmm, I don't know. Do you have a swimsuit?"

A sad look filled her little face. "No."

"Ah. Well, when it gets warmer, we'll buy you a swimsuit and you can play in the creek with Daisy."

Megan could've told him Torie wouldn't forget his promise. She hoped he hadn't made it lightly.

The child began jumping up and down. "I can? Really?" Rick nodded and Torie spun on her toes and raced for the kitchen door, calling, "Grandma! Grandma! Guess what?"

"She won't forget."

Rick looked at her, a question in his eyes. "I didn't think she would."

"Good. Because every day she's going to ask if it's warm enough to play in the creek."

"That's okay. At least she won't stare at me like I'm some kind of monster."

Megan blinked. She hadn't realized he'd noticed Torie's wariness. "I'm sorry. It's not you. She's—"

"Been frightened by her father?"

Megan nodded but said nothing.

"I won't ever hurt her, Megan. You know that, don't you? I may not know much about kids, but I know they don't deserve to be frightened."

"Thank you," she whispered. "You're doing fine with Torie." She hurriedly wiped away the moisture from her eyes. "Ready for some chocolate cake? We need to finish it off because Mother is dying to bake something else for you."

"I think your mother should open a restaurant. She's a great cook." He rose and carried his dinner plate to the sink.

Megan jumped up. "I can clear the table."

"I told you before, Megan, I'm not asking to be waited on hand and foot."

His sharp tone surprised her. His voice had been so gentle when he was talking with Torie. Instead of questioning him, she cut two pieces of the rich chocolate cake and carried them to the table. "I'm going to get some milk to go with my cake. Do you want some?"

"I don't know if I have any milk," he said with a frown.

"We brought some."

"I'll give you some money for it," he said, nodding to her.

"Why?"

"Because you don't need to be buying food. That's my job." He took a big bite of cake and smiled in satisfaction. Then he added, "I'll set up an account for you and your mother to use for shopping."

"No, we can pay for our food. We're living here free. There's no reason—"

"I'm the husband, Megan. It's my job to provide for my family."

"We're a pretend family, Rick. I will pay for our food. After all, I'm working."

"No, you won't," he thundered, apparently having lost patience with her arguing.

"Whatever's the matter?" Faith asked, coming into the kitchen, carrying Torie.

Megan saw the anxious look on the child's face and immediately fell silent.

Rick, too, seemed to realize they were upsetting the child. "Nothing's wrong," he said and managed a smile, which was more than Megan could do. "I'm going to set up an account tomorrow to pay for things."

Faith looked at him blankly, as if she had no conception of what he could be talking about.

"The groceries, Faith. And things the kids need. I don't want you or Megan feeling you have to ask me for money, or pay for things yourself."

"Tell him, Mom. He can't do that."

"Yes, I can. Not only can, I *will* do that."

"But you—"

"My goodness," Faith interrupted. "You two aren't thinking."

Rick frowned so fiercely that Megan almost laughed. The man didn't like criticism.

"Of course I'm thinking," he insisted, though his tone wasn't as fierce as it had been. "I'm thinking I need to take care of my family."

"And that's a lovely thought, and more than we deserve," Faith assured him, patting his shoulder. "And I know Megan was protesting because she feels you've already given us so much."

Megan nodded, pleading with her gaze for Rick to understand.

"But instead of shouting at each other, you need to compromise." Faith soothed Torie as she continued. "We'll put some money in the fund and so will you. There will be plenty and we'll all be contributing."

"There's no need—" Rick began.

"Yes, there is," Megan interrupted. "We don't want to cause you to run short on taking care of the ranch. I know you don't have a big budget, or you would've already hired a housekeeper."

He looked uncomfortable and Megan supposed he was embarrassed by his financial situation. But the man was a hard worker. Sometimes, Mother Nature didn't reward you as she should.

"We're going to save a lot of our money for the legal bills, Rick, but there will be some left over. We want to contribute to our living expenses." Megan smiled at the big man, something she should've remembered to do all along. Her mother was right to remind her that Rick was doing something important for them. She needed to be sure he knew she appreciated his sacrifices.

Rick stared at both her and her mother. Finally, he nodded and turned his attention to the cake. "Fine. I'll open the account tomorrow."

With a satisfied nod, Faith moved over to the sink and sat Torie on the counter. "Have we finished the chocolate cake? Rick, what would you like me to make next? I bake a lovely peach cobbler. Do you like cobbler?"

"Yes, ma'am," he agreed, and Megan could tell he was already distracted from their argument. "There's nothing better than hot cobbler with ice cream melting on top of it."

His gaze had become dreamy, as if he were tasting that dish right now. Megan chuckled. If she wanted Rick Astin's attention, not that she did, of course, she'd have to turn herself into a tasty dish.

Maybe a strawberry shortcake.

MEGAN HAD HER morning free. She and her mother did the last-minute packing. Everything else was already in place for them to move to Rick's.

"You should be going to the beauty shop, having breakfast in bed, like Andrea—" Faith stopped, a stricken look on her face.

Megan bit her bottom lip, holding back the words that said she didn't want to do anything like her big sister had, particularly anything to do with her marriage. But her mother didn't need that reminder.

"Don't worry, Mom. Next time I'll have breakfast in bed."

Her mother muttered something under her breath, but Megan didn't understand the words. When she asked for clarification, Faith, her cheeks bright red, said it didn't matter.

Megan was reminded of what had happened two nights earlier with her car. "Mom? Did anyone…no, never mind." She couldn't ask that question. It sounded ridiculous. "It's time for me to go in to work. Do you have everything under control here?"

"Yes, I do. But hurry home. The wedding starts at seven, you know."

Megan bit her lip again before giving her mother a smile and slipping out the door. Like she'd forget that she was marrying a stranger this evening! That wasn't a normal occurrence in a woman's life.

At least it shouldn't be.

A picture of Rick Astin popped into her head. He was the epitome of a romantic hero. Broad shouldered, narrow hipped, a handsome smile. She remembered his gentleness with Torie. He more than looked like a hero. He acted like one. At least he had so far.

The future, however, frightened her. When Andrea had married Drake, they had all thought the future looked bright. True, he hadn't interested Megan. She'd thought Drake was a little heavy-handed, but her mother accused her of being too independent. But even then, Megan hadn't realized how Drake would change.

So, even though Rick seemed like a nice man, Megan would hold back a judgment.

"You're being ridiculous," she said to herself, as she parked the car by the clinic. "It doesn't matter, because you're not really going to be married. It's a temporary thing."

That comforting thought made it possible to put a smile on her face.

RICK SPENT THE morning of his wedding day doing his usual work. He surveyed the calf he'd just discovered in the back pasture, already nursing, with satisfaction. His crop of calves was exceeding his expectations.

He'd made all kinds of projections on the computer, planning his year as a rancher. But he knew paper expectations could go to hell in a handbasket if Mother Nature decided not to cooperate.

But the bull he'd chosen and purchased was giving him strong babies. Black Boy hadn't had much of a track record, which is why he got him for the price he did, but he was really paying off.

Jose rode over. "Another healthy one?"

"Looks like it."

"We'd better move the mothers and babies closer in. I heard there's a pack of coyotes that have been killing calves in the area."

"Where'd you hear that?"

"At the bar last night. One of the cowboys from the Marcus spread was talking about it."

"Okay, we'll move this pair into the next pasture. Then I'll see Tuck and Spence tonight and ask if they've had any problems." His spread was between the two men and they'd become friends since his move to Cactus. The two experienced ranchers had offered advice and assistance when he'd needed it.

"Is there a party tonight?" Jose asked.

Rick frowned. He hadn't thought about asking anyone to the wedding. Tuck and Spence would be there because of their mothers, friends of Faith. "Well, sort of. I forgot to mention that I'm…" Somehow the words stuck in his throat. He'd never expected to say them again. He cleared his throat and managed to say, "I'm getting married tonight."

His cowhand stared at him. "You forgot?"

"Um, I didn't forget that I was getting married, but I didn't—I haven't been much involved in planning it. Tuck and Spence will be there because Ruth and Edith, their mothers, are helping with it. Can you come?"

"You sure you want me to come? I mean, if it's just family…"

"Hell, Jose, I don't have any family. You can be my family. Find a pretty lady and come on. We're to be at the church by seven. Then we'll have dinner at The Last Roundup."

"Hey, I'll be there. Congratulations, man!"

"Yeah, thanks." Congratulations to him. Congratulations to repeating the biggest mistake of his life.

MEGAN DIDN'T get home from the clinic until almost six o'clock. Samantha apologized for keeping her so late, but they had an emergency come in at the last minute.

"Don't worry about it," Megan assured her. "They can't have a wedding without the bride, so they'll just have to wait."

"I know," Samantha assured her. "But Florence will be upset."

Megan had been here long enough to know better. "Your mother-in-law thinks you walk on water, you fraud. She'll know it wasn't your fault."

Samantha beamed. "I know. She's so wonderful."

With a sigh, Megan stowed away the last of the supplies they'd used. "Okay, I'm done. I'll hurry home and turn into a blushing bride. Then I'll be back at nine in the morning."

Samantha shook her head.

"Nope. It's a surprise, but Marybelle agreed to

work all day tomorrow so you can have the day off.''

"No!'' Megan protested. ''That's not necessary.''

"Oh, yes, it is,'' Samantha assured her, with a look that made Megan uneasy.

Chapter Six

Rick swallowed his nervousness, trying to give the appearance of an eager bridegroom. Instead of a man facing the gallows. *Get a grip, man. This isn't for real.*

"You okay?" Cal Baxter asked. He was standing next to Rick, as his best man.

Giving the best grin he could summon, Rick muttered, "Yeah, of course."

It amazed him, as the organ music began, how quickly the ladies of Cactus had pulled together a real wedding. He'd assumed he and Megan would stand up in front of the preacher, say their vows, and be done. Instead, he was wearing a tux, there were flowers everywhere, and, damn it, there were a lot of people in the church.

Where had they come from?

He'd invited Jose, of course, who was sitting in the second row, a very attractive young woman beside him. And Cal's wife had agreed to be Megan's maid of honor. Then, the four matchmakers and

their husbands were in attendance, along with Faith
and Torie and Drew.

And, of course, Tuck and Spence, with their families, and Mac, the attorney Megan had consulted,
whose mother Florence was one of the matchmakers.

But the others? He recognized the feed store man
who'd introduced Megan to him. That must be his
wife beside him. And Lucy, the one from the drugstore—

A sudden shifting of the man beside him caught
Rick's attention, halting his inventory of the guests.
He followed Cal's line of vision and realized the
music had changed and Jessica, in a blue suit, was
coming down the aisle.

Envy filled him. Not because of Jessica's beauty,
or because he had any interest in her romantically,
but because of the marriage she had with Cal.
They'd been married over a year and a half, and
you'd think it was *their* wedding day.

He found it hard to believe there were marriages
like theirs, especially after going through one himself, but they were living proof.

His own marriage had been a mistake almost
from the first day of the honeymoon. He'd tried and
tried to remember what had prompted him to think
they could make a go of it, but he remained bewil-
dered.

Then suddenly his breath deserted him.

Megan.

His bride.

She was dressed in a cream suit that hugged her curves and gave her an air of sophistication that belied the dinners they'd shared in his kitchen. Softening the look, however, was a cream rosebud and baby's breath tucked in her hair.

The perfect bride.

He quickly reminded himself that his first bride had looked elegant also. Of course, he'd paid for it. In more ways than one.

But this bride was temporary. So, if she turned out to be less than she looked on their wedding day, it wouldn't cost him anything. He could breathe again.

And took a deep breath.

Lordy, she was beautiful, though.

MEGAN CAUGHT HER breath as she looked down the aisle at the man waiting to become her husband.

She'd thought him handsome, sexy, in tight jeans and a Stetson. But in a tux, he was incredible. *A tux? How had he had time to get a tux? He probably had to go into Lubbock, an hour's drive away.*

She felt badly that he'd taken that much time out from his busy schedule. A tux hadn't been necessary. But the man seemed determined to do everything right. Even if it was a pretend wedding.

Vowing to repay his every kindness and consideration in whatever way she could, Megan took a deep breath and continued toward the altar. She walked alone.

Letting someone "give" her away bothered her.

If and when she ever married for real, it would be because she wanted to unite with a man. Her choice.

One she didn't think she'd ever make.

Her gaze met with Rick's and relief flooded her. His eyes weren't filled with love. Or even lust. She held back the chuckle that rose in her. Thank goodness she'd learn to read his eyes. Because they were filled with stark terror, just like her own. Nothing could've reassured her more.

She stepped to his side, trying to smile. The man was helping them out. He musnt't suffer because of his charity.

All through the ceremony, concern for Rick made Megan's role easier to perform. She tried to put the man at ease. A gentle squeeze of his flesh when the pastor asked them to join hands seemed to ease his strain. Her smile as she said her vows, as if inviting him to share the amusement of their situation, brought an answering smile.

In fact, Megan was feeling quite relaxed. She was certain she was doing the right thing, since it wasn't real, by the time they finished the ceremony.

Until the pastor said those traditional words she'd forgotten about.

"You may kiss the bride."

OKAY, RICK ADMITTED, that was one part of the wedding he didn't mind. Kissing the bride. He'd thought about kissing Megan. Dreamed of kissing Megan. Hungered to kiss Megan.

Of course, he would've preferred not to kiss her for the first time in front of a large audience. But, hey, a guy had to do what a guy had to do.

He wrapped his arms around her slender form and slowly lowered his lips to hers. A perfect fit. No awkwardness, no fumbling, no...reserve. The kiss was incredible, the best he'd ever experienced. The lady was a great kisser. And he didn't want to stop.

Until Cal put a hand on his shoulder and tugged. "Whoa, cowboy, come up for air."

He stared at his friend, frowning, until his gaze trailed away to their audience. Then he quickly turned to Megan, ready to apologize.

The stunned look on her face made him think better of wasting words. He slipped his arm back around her and pulled her tightly against him as the pastor introduced them as husband and wife.

"Smile," he whispered to her, hoping to wipe that panic from her face. He was relieved when her lips widened, even if the smile was weak.

"What do we do now?" he whispered to Cal. He wasn't doing much better than Megan.

Cal chuckled. "You lead your bride back up the aisle. There'll be a car waiting for you at the door. Tuck's dad is driving you to the restaurant in his Cadillac."

"You're coming, too, aren't you?" Rick asked, panic filling him at the idea of being alone with Megan. He figured she'd take him to task for his enthusiastic kiss.

Cal, after a pause, nodded. "Sure, Jess and I can ride with you...if that's what you want."

"Yeah." Then Rick followed instructions, pulling a silent Megan along with him as they walked up the aisle, past the smiling crowd.

As Cal had predicted, Frank Langford was waiting on the sidewalk, beaming at them. As they approached, he swept open the backdoor.

"Thanks, Mr. Langford," Rick muttered as first Megan and then he ducked and entered the spacious car.

Cal bent over and stuck his head in. "Sure you want us to come with you? It will make it a little crowded."

"Yeah, we want you to come. We'll make room." Without consulting his bride, Rick reached over and lifted her into his lap. Then he scooted against the window.

"Rick—" Megan shrieked, clutching at his shoulder with one hand during the transfer, while the other held her bouquet.

Jessica slid into the car, distracting Megan, followed by Cal. She grinned at them. "That's a good way to conserve space."

Rick didn't think so. He figured he was going to need some more space in his tuxedo pants if the ride was a long one. But fortunately, he knew the restaurant was only a couple of blocks away, on the town square.

Much to his relief, Jessica chatted about the wedding during their short trip.

"What a beautiful wedding!" Jessica enthused. "Isn't it amazing what those women can do in a hurry? I guess they've had so much practice now, it's becoming quite routine. Was everything okay, Megan?"

"It was lovely," she said softly.

Rick couldn't help tightening his hold around her waist. Okay, so their marriage wasn't real. He was still her husband until she decided otherwise. It was his job to support her.

"Yeah, and the bride was beautiful," Rick said, just as softly. Then he abruptly remembered the couple beside him. "And the matron of honor, too."

"No argument here," Cal assured him, hugging Jessica to him. She laid her head on his shoulder, and Rick wished Megan would do the same.

On *his* shoulder, he meant.

Just for appearances, of course.

It was a relief to discover they'd reached the restaurant. Putting some distance between him and Megan would be a good idea.

Before he kissed her again.

Once they were out of the car, with Frank promising to return as soon as he parked, Rick looked at Cal, his guide.

"Do we go anywhere in particular? I mean, is there a table reserved or—"

"Man, you don't know anything, do you?" Cal teased. "The entire dance hall is reserved. There's a band and everything. Jess has set up a buffet and there's a huge wedding cake.''

Rick stared at his friend. ''All the people from the church are coming?''

Jessica laughed. ''Every last one of them. It's the way we do things here.''

He sneaked a quick look at Megan and then nodded to his friends. ''Okay. Well, let's go.''

Jessica's restaurant, the most popular one in Cactus, had a large room to the right of the main dining room that had a small stage. On weekend nights, the room was opened and local bands had an opportunity to show their stuff.

Tonight, as Cal had said, it was a reception hall with a large wedding cake occupying the place of honor on the buffet table. With his arm still around Megan, Rick led her over to look at the delicate roses in cream, nestled among green leaves on all four layers.

On top of the cake, a bride and groom stood arm in arm, both with dark hair and smiles.

Megan reached out one shaky finger to touch the pair, as if to be sure they were really there.

Before Rick could think of anything to say, the first of the guests arrived and Jessica herded them to the door to form a mini-reception line to greet them.

Rick did his duty, shaking hands and smiling at his neighbors, but it wasn't nearly as much fun as kissing the bride.

MEGAN WAS still in shock.

She'd recognized the attraction she felt for Rick Astin. But she'd assured herself it wouldn't be a problem. After all, it was lust. She'd felt it before, sort of. She'd been attracted to a few men.

But she'd never given in to it.

When Rick kissed her at the altar, she'd prepared herself for a brief meeting of their lips. She'd even admit now that she'd been looking forward to it.

Idiot!

The man was an incredible kisser. The James Bond of all kissers. Or maybe it was just that her experience was so limited. What did it matter? The point was she was in trouble.

Because she wanted him to kiss her again.

And that mustn't happen.

Now that they were out of the car, she could put some distance between them, concentrate on other things. She shook hands with all the strangers, only a few of whom she'd met before. She concentrated on their names and faces.

It kept her from concentrating on her husband.

Husband. That word sent shivers through her.

Rick leaned toward her. ''Are you all right? Are you cold?''

She shook her head, stiffening her shoulders. He'd felt her shiver? She obviously hadn't put enough distance between them. From now on, she'd make sure he didn't touch her.

''Ladies and gentlemen,'' a booming voice said

from the small stage. "It's time for our newlyweds to lead the first dance."

"No!" Megan mumbled, her eyes widening.

Rick wrapped that strong arm around her waist again and led her toward the center of the room. "Don't worry. They don't expect Fred and Ginger."

She guessed she should be grateful he didn't realize what she'd meant by her protest. She sucked in a deep breath and tried to hold it through the dance, as if that would stop him from touching her.

Instead, he cuddled her closer. "Relax, Meg. It's just a dance."

Just a dance. And that kiss had just been a kiss. And their marriage was just a marriage.

And she was just an idiot. She couldn't do this. She couldn't share a house with this man, a life with this man, without paying a heavy price.

"Rick," she began, thinking maybe they should get an annulment before—no, it couldn't be too late for an annulment because they weren't going to make this a real marriage. That's right, it was a pretend marriage.

The kiss had almost made her forget that important fact. It wasn't a real marriage.

His lips brushed across hers, dragging her gaze to him. "Don't do that! Don't…you can't—"

"But everyone's watching. Don't you want them to believe this is a love match?" When she stared at him blankly, he added, "For the children? Isn't that what you said?"

"Y-Yes, for the children." Dear God, she'd almost forgotten why she was doing this, marrying this stranger. She'd almost panicked and called the whole thing off because his kiss, his touch, had made her forget the reality.

She sought her mother in the group of people sitting down at the tables, watching them. There she was, holding a sleepy Torie. Drew was in a neighbor's arms, already asleep.

The children. She had to protect her sister's children. And Rick was helping her do that. He'd been magnificent, doing everything and more that she'd asked him to do.

"Yes, you're right," she said with a sigh, leaning her head against his strong shoulder. "We need to pretend... for the children."

He pulled her even more tightly against him. "It's not so hard, is it? We fit together well."

She gave a small nod and closed her eyes. It was best if she didn't think about that. She'd concentrate on the children.

AFTER THAT first dance Rick found his bride in great demand. So much so, that he didn't even get close to her for the next hour. But he kept his gaze fixed on her.

Finally, Jessica ordered him to grab Megan and come cut the cake. "After you do that, you both need to eat something."

"Okay, I won't argue with that."

He strode across the dance floor and tapped Ed

Baxter on his shoulder. "Time for us to cut the cake, Mr. Baxter."

"Well, I guess I can give up the rest of my dance for such a good cause, but don't you forget, young lady. You owe me half a dance."

"I won't forget, Mr. Baxter," Megan said softly, a gentle smile on her lips.

Which made Rick want to kiss her again.

Hell, he had half a million reasons to kiss her again. He'd collected them as he'd watched her dance around the room in the arms of other men.

"Are you any good at cutting a big cake, 'cause I don't have any idea how to go about it," he told her as they moved in that direction.

"We only have to cut one piece," she assured him, taking his hand in hers. It was the first time she'd voluntarily touched him tonight, except when she'd rested her head on his shoulder during that one dance.

"I'll let you show me," he assured her, realizing the way to his wife's heart—no, not her heart, her kindness. The way to receive consideration from her was to need her.

But not in the way he needed her.

Florence Greenfield, Mac's aunt, was in charge of the cake, and she directed them on cutting the first piece.

"Now, you each feed the other a bite. And I don't want anyone smushing cake on the other's face. That's a barbarian thing to do," Florence instructed.

"Yes, ma'am," Rick agreed, smiling at Megan. He broke off a small bite of the cake and offered it to Megan.

With an embarrassed look, she leaned forward and took the cake into her mouth, along with his fingers. Rick thought he'd died and gone to heaven as her tongue flicked his skin.

When she picked up a slightly larger piece of cake and lifted it to him, he reached out and clasped her wrist. After taking in the cake, he licked her fingers. Her cheeks flushed and their guests cheered. Then he followed up that display with another kiss. A sweet, sensual tasting of her and the wedding cake that was ambrosia.

When he lifted his head, his gaze caught a flick of icing on her upper lip and he couldn't resist touching her lips with his tongue.

"Rick!" she protested, her cheeks red.

"Icing," he assured her even as he stared at her face, hoping for another reason.

"Nicely done," Florence said, interrupting their concentration on each other. "Now, go fill your plates at the buffet while everyone else eats cake."

"She is definitely a mother…or a general," Rick muttered with a grin as they followed her directions.

"She and the others have been so helpful since we moved back here. It's meant a lot to Mom."

"Yeah," he agreed, but he hadn't forgotten the disconnected battery cable. They needed to be on their toes.

"Oh! I forgot to tell you. I asked Samantha if you could participate in the roundups so they'd come help you with yours. I mean, Tuck and Spence and—"

"I'd already made that arrangement," he told her, surprised that she'd interfere in his ranch work.

"Oh. I...I wanted to help you. You've done so much for us."

"It's a mutual thing, Megan. You and your mom are doing a lot for me, too. Here, have some brisket."

Distractedly, she let him fill her plate. "How did you know about the roundups? You haven't been here that long."

"I moved here as they were starting the fall roundups. I offered to help out, even though I wasn't ready for one. I figured it would help me meet folks, get to know the area."

"Oh. That was very smart of you."

"I appreciate you thinking of me, though," he said and leaned over to kiss her again. He'd planned just a brief kiss, a thank-you kiss. But the second his lips touched hers, he lost control.

"Watch out! You're going to spill your plates!" someone warned and he jerked back.

"Uh, yeah, thanks." It was a good thing the reception wouldn't last much longer, because he was becoming addicted to kissing Megan Ford. Megan Astin. Her name was Megan Astin. At least that was real.

"Come on, let's sit down," he suggested.

While they ate, the cake was served to the guests and the noise of the gathering simmered to a low level as everyone consumed the cake.

Before the evening ended, however, the band returned to the stand and played a riff of announcement music and Mabel Baxter walked to the microphone.

Rick frowned. He'd thought the evening was winding down. He'd figured he and Megan would take their family home and go to their separate bedrooms, leaving him unsatisfied but safe.

Separate from her.

"Ladies and gentlemen!" Mabel said, gathering everyone's attention. Then she said, "Rick and Megan. Usually, everyone arrives at a wedding with gifts. But since you both already have house things, we decided to do something different for your wedding."

He and Megan exchanged wary glances before turning their attention back to Mabel.

"What you don't have is a honeymoon." Before they could say anything, Mabel held up her hands to stop them. "I know, I know. Megan is supposed to work and there's the children. So, Marybelle has agreed to work for you tomorrow, Megan. You can sleep in," Mabel assured her, suggesting with her tone that Megan might be doing something besides sleeping.

Everyone laughed.

Except for Megan and Rick.

"Our housekeeper has agreed to spend the night

with Faith at the house, to take care of the children,'' Mabel continued. ''And the reason for that is because you and Rick are going to have at least one honeymoon night. You two have a reservation at the bed and breakfast across the square for a night in their honeymoon suite, including breakfast in bed in the morning!''

Everyone cheered.

Everyone except for Megan and Rick.

Chapter Seven

"Isn't it wonderful?" Faith enthused as she ran to Megan's side to hug her.

Her mother's action awakened Megan from the frozen state she'd been in since Mabel's announcement. "Mom, how could you let them—you *know* we don't want that!" she whispered.

Faith leaned back. "It's so wonderful because two people in *love* as much as you are deserve a little privacy, a little celebration."

Megan read the message in Faith's words and gaze. It was supposed to be a love match. She shifted her gaze to Rick. He'd been watching her mother, too.

"Speech! Speech!" someone in the crowd shouted.

Rick reached out and took her hand, sending her a look that told her he'd gotten Faith's message. Helping Megan to her feet, he led her over to the stage. They stepped up and he pulled her against him, his arm around her waist, and held up a hand to stop the cheering.

"Folks, this community is the best! You've made both of us feel welcome. And I can guarantee you this is one wedding present that won't be returned!" Then he leaned down and gave Megan another of those mind-numbing kisses.

All she could do was cooperate to the best of her ability. Which wasn't all that much since he'd kissed her. But their audience seemed to believe all was well. They were busy preparing for the bride and groom's departure. Edith Hauk stepped to the stage holding Megan's wedding bouquet.

"Time to find a new bride, Megan. Turn your back and toss it. Single ladies, come closer."

There was a rush of ladies of all ages.

Rick whispered in her ear. "Looks like not everyone thinks marriage is a disaster."

No. Not everyone. Just the bride and groom.

Megan turned her back and tossed the flowers into the air. Amid a lot of squealing and grabbing, a blushing young woman held the bouquet aloft in triumph.

"Now the garter," Edith insisted.

Megan stared at her blankly.

"You did put on the garter, didn't you?" Edith asked. "We sent it over. Faith promised you'd wear it."

She had worn it, because her mother had insisted, but Megan had forgotten about that tradition. She nodded, wishing she hadn't pushed it so high.

"Kneel down, Rick, and take it off," Edith ordered.

He did as he was told and slid big warm hands up her right leg.

"The other leg!" Megan hissed, trying to hide the shivers his touch caused.

The grin he sent her told her he was enjoying this part of the evening more than he should. She vowed revenge, though she wasn't sure how she'd be able to wreak it.

As she caught her breath, he'd slid the blue, lace-trimmed garter down her leg. "Lift your foot, sweetheart."

By the time he stood, the single men had been pushed to the forefront. Several of them seemed a lot less eager than the women. Rick turned his back and tossed the garter. It flew through the air and landed in a hapless fellow's hands in the back of the crowd, surprising him more than anyone.

"Hey! I don't intend to—I'm not getting married!" he protested amid laughter.

Megan couldn't resist a quick look at Rick. After all, that had been his attitude, too.

He gave her a wink, as if he knew what she was thinking. But, of course, he didn't. He didn't know her that well. Then she remembered how well she thought she understood him when their gazes had met at the altar.

He surprised her again, stepping from the stage and then sweeping her into his arms.

"Rick!" she protested in his ear, sure no one could hear her amid the cheers. "What are you doing?"

He didn't bother to answer. Striding to the door, amid well wishes and rose petals the guests had received to shower on them, he made a beeline for the exit.

"We need to get out of here before they come up with any more ideas," he told her as he reached the front porch.

"Yes, but I can walk. You can't carry me across the square. That's too far."

"I think I could manage it," he protested, as if she'd insulted his manhood.

She squirmed. "We can go faster if I walk. Here they come!" she warned as the crowd surged after them.

He set her on her feet and took her hand. Though she had on heels, they weren't high, and she managed to keep up with him as they ran across the square. Only the hardy continued to follow, but even they stopped when Rick and Megan reached the front door of the bed and breakfast.

The hostess was waiting for them and showed them to the honeymoon suite on the second floor with a big smile on her face. "Enjoy yourselves!" she trilled as she closed the door behind them.

HELL! What was he supposed to do now?

Not that Rick would need directions if this was his real honeymoon. Retrieving the garter had warmed him up for what he'd—whoa, this wasn't real.

No honeymoon.

"Uh, Megan—"

"What are we going to do?" she demanded as she whirled to face him. She looked like she was about to cry.

"Sweetheart, don't get upset. We'll…we'll manage. And you'll have to admit, it does make the wedding look real."

He couldn't believe he was seconding the actions of the matchmakers. He had no doubt they were the ones behind the wedding gift.

"But we don't…I mean, I don't even have a toothbrush!"

He couldn't hold back a lopsided smile. If it were a real honeymoon, a toothbrush would be about all he'd be concerned about. No need for clothes.

Just the thought of Megan without her beautiful suit, her lacy lingerie, made Rick salivate. He immediately shut that thought down. His tux was well-tailored and didn't leave a lot of room to disguise his reaction.

Megan, still holding her bouquet that had been returned to her after the toss, began to pace the room. "I can't believe Mom let them do this. I don't care how good it makes our marriage look. She could've at least warned us."

"They probably swore her to secrecy. Look, it's not so bad. There are two rooms. I'll sleep out here, on the sofa, and you can have the bedroom. Then, in the morning, we'll go home."

He was relieved when she seemed to settle down. Drawing a deep breath, she turned to face him.

"I'm sorry, Rick. I know this is as hard for you as it is for me. I...I was just so...I felt so betrayed by my own mother. I didn't really believe you about the car."

The urge to wrap her in his arms, to comfort her, to remove the sense of betrayal he could see in her eyes, almost overcame him. He even took a step in her direction, but the alarm in her gaze stopped him.

"Let's, uh, let's check out the digs. See if you'll be comfortable." He walked past her and opened the door on the other side of the room.

And sighed.

A king-size bed with fluffy pillows, the cover turned back with pale blue sheets, looked so inviting, he groaned.

"What is it?" Megan demanded, pressing herself against him and peeking around. "Oh."

"Yeah," he agreed and cleared his throat. "Uh, I think you'll be comfortable." Oh, yeah. And if he joined her... Another thought to be suppressed.

He wanted to back up, to avoid stepping into that seductive bower. Fresh roses in a crystal vase perfumed the room and soft lighting completed the picture. The old-fashioned cutglass lamp lent a magical air.

Megan was still pressed against his back, eliminating the possibility of retreat.

"Is that your luggage?"

His head snapped up and he frowned. "What luggage?"

She pointed to a chair by the window where three

leather bags, obviously expensive, rested, stacked one on top of the other.

"No, that's not my luggage."

"Mine, neither."

She skirted around him and approached the luggage. Then she stopped and turned back to him. "Don't you think we should see whose it is?"

Which meant, of course, that he had to enter the room.

"Uh, sure."

He crossed the room, keeping as far from the bed as possible. By that time, Megan had opened the overnight bag and found a card.

With a shaky voice, she read,

"Dear Megan and Rick,
Everyone wanted to contribute to your wedding gift and we received much more than the honeymoon suite costs, so we bought this luggage and a few things for the night. Enjoy!"

"What other things?" he asked. He was worried about what the matchmakers might've come up with.

"I don't know. There's nothing else in here," Megan assured him. She secured the lid and set the suitcase over on the bed, then reached for the medium-size bag.

When she opened it, all Rick saw was a filmy blue gown that immediately fired up his imagination again.

All he needed.

He took a step back. "Uh, looks like it's stuff for you."

She lifted a pair of black silk briefs. "I think these would be for you."

He snatched them out of her hand. "Uh, yeah. That's great. I'll take a shower." A cold one.

"Here's some jeans and a shirt, your boots," she said, digging through the suitcase. "I don't see any pajamas."

Rick snorted, unable to control his humor. "No, I guess not. I don't wear pajamas."

He watched in fascination as her cheeks heated up.

"Oh."

"Is there a change of clothes for you?" he quickly asked, hoping to relieve her embarrassment.

"Yes." She lifted a dress from the bag and held it against her. It wasn't formal like her suit. He could tell it was going to cling to her, softly enhancing her curves.

Underneath the dress was some lacy underwear. When Megan realized that, she dropped the dress back to the suitcase and slammed the lid. "Everything I need."

"Okay," he agreed, clearing his throat again. "Good." He reached up and untied the tux's bow tie. It was getting too tight.

His action caught her attention. "I didn't know you were going to wear a tux. Thank you. I'm sorry you had to take so much time to get one."

He frowned. "Time? It didn't take any time."

"Didn't you have to drive into Lubbock?"

Still distracted by her beauty, he shook his head no and added, "Cal and I both had them."

She frowned at him.

"Well, if you've got everything you need, I'll, uh, see you in the morning."

He began backing away from her, but she stopped him.

"The bathroom is in there, if you want—you can go first." She lifted the lid and reached back into the suitcase. "Here's your toothbrush."

He grabbed it and was on his way to the bathroom when he heard a gasp. He spun around. "What is it?"

"Nothing!" she protested, but her cheeks were bright red.

"Megan?" He moved in her direction and she held up a hand.

It took him a minute to realize she was holding a package of condoms. "Man, they really did think of everything."

"I can't believe—"

Rick chuckled. "Just picture one of those ladies purchasing those condoms. That I would've paid to see."

Megan tried to hide her amusement, but her lips quivered with laughter. "They probably were as comfortable as I would be."

"Ah. So you're not a swinger?"

Megan didn't think she could be more embarrassed. "No!"

"I didn't think so, or I wouldn't be sleeping on the couch," he said with a gentle smile.

"I can take the couch if you think you'll be uncomfortable."

"No, sweetheart, I'll take the couch." Then he entered the bathroom, closing the door behind him.

Megan stood there, staring at the closed door, startled by the regret that filled her. She'd never been a believer in sexual promiscuity. So why was she wishing she could throw her caution and restraint out the window now?

Because her bridegroom was a sexy man. And a great kisser. That was all. It was lust. And that wasn't a good reason to break her promises to herself. But it certainly was a temptation.

She sank onto the bed with a sigh. All she could do was wait for Rick to return to the living room. The only nightgown in the suitcase was that sheer, frothy thing that hid nothing from view. She certainly couldn't put that on until she had absolute privacy.

The door to the bathroom opened and Megan sprang to her feet, as if sitting on the bed in Rick's presence was too dangerous.

"I'm going to wait until morning for my shower," he explained. Keeping his distance from the bed, he edged his way to the door. "I'll see you in the morning."

"Wait!" she called and then took a step back as he spun around, an eager expression on his face.

"You'll need a pillow and some cover."

His arms were full with his change of clothes and toothbrush, so Megan gathered the pillow and one of the blankets from the foot of the bed and came toward him. "I'll fix your bed for you."

"I can manage."

"It's the least I can do," she assured him, concerned about the roughness of his voice. Was he angry with her?

They both walked into the sitting room and Megan eyed the couch, as a bed for Rick, for the first time. It was an antique settee. It didn't even look comfortable for sitting, much less sleeping.

"You can't sleep here," she said flatly.

"I'll manage," he grumbled. Putting his load down on the coffee table, he reached for the bedding.

But she clutched it to her chest. "I'm serious, Rick. You'll be up all night."

He glared at her. "I probably will be anyway."

"Why? Aren't you tired?"

"Damn it, Megan, don't you know anything about men?" he demanded, his hands on his hips, the tuxedo shirt unbuttoned halfway.

Megan thought he'd never looked more handsome. But she did know something about men, and a closer examination told her that he was aroused.

"Oh."

He gave her a wry grin. "Yeah. So I'll sleep here."

"But I'm shorter. I could—"

"No!"

Suddenly, she'd reached her limit. "Fine! Be hardheaded and suffer! See if I care." She dropped the bedding at his feet and stormed back into the bedroom, slamming the door behind her.

Then leaned against the door, her shoulders sagging, feeling sorry for herself and her husband. They were doing the right thing, trying to protect Torie and Drew. Why did the right thing have to be so painful?

Slowly, she prepared for bed, her limbs heavy as her thoughts dwelled on Rick. When she donned the negligee, it's silky folds sliding over her skin, she couldn't help going to the bathroom to stare in the mirror.

She liked the way she looked and wished—no, she couldn't share her pleasure with Rick. Then she would be a tease. Rick was suffering enough with that ridiculous excuse for a sofa in the next room.

Sliding into the big, comfortable bed, she felt doubly guilty as she continued to think of Rick. There was plenty of room. But the reminder he'd given her when she'd insisted he couldn't sleep there kept her still.

Their marriage was not real. They were going through all this for the children. She should be thinking about Torie and Drew instead of Rick.

She tried. She pictured Torie playing house, having a tea party with her dollies and Aunt Megan. Cuddling up in her arms. Drew, pulling himself up, so proud of his accomplishment before landing on his bottom, a look of surprise on his face.

Those thoughts brought a smile to her face and a relaxation to her body. But as she turned on her side and clutched the pillow closer, the last thought she had was that of her handsome husband kissing her at the altar.

IT WAS A rough night.

Rick tried to get comfortable on the sofa from hell. It might as well have been a bed of nails.

He'd stripped to his underwear, in hopes of getting some sleep. That hadn't helped.

Then he'd gotten up and paced for an hour, figuring he'd tire himself out. Once he'd even gently opened the door to the bedroom. In the shadows, he saw Megan curled up under the cover, her beautiful hair spread across the pillow, sleeping peacefully.

He'd closed the door and muttered a few curse words.

Not to Megan. It wasn't her fault she was such an innocent, undisturbed by the events of the day. She hadn't had a bad marriage.

He remembered the panic he'd felt at the altar, and her warm touch that distracted him. He grinned. She'd been trying to reassure him. And had. His ex-wife hadn't had a single thought for anyone but herself from their wedding day on.

Megan was different. She married for the children. And she was concerned about his feelings. And she turned him on like no other woman.

He'd slept with his wife before their wedding. He had been attracted to her. But it was nothing compared to what he felt when he kissed Megan.

He should've kissed her before the wedding.

Then he would've known he couldn't marry her. It made him want her too much. And the more he kissed her, the more he wanted her.

He'd keep his distance from now on. Taking care of his herd, his ranch, that would distract him. Until he rode in at night to find Megan waiting for him in a clean house, good food on the table, a smile on her lips.

He groaned.

Hell, he was going to be in a constant fight with his hormones.

Weariness suddenly filled him. With a wrathful glare at the sofa, he sank onto it and sighed. He never had liked antiques. Now he hated them.

Doubling his knees up so his feet didn't hang off the end, he covered himself with the blanket. At least the pillow was comfortable.

He gradually drifted off, only to reawaken every time he extended his legs. He'd punch his pillow and settle again. Only to awaken again.

And each time he came to, his mind traveled a few feet into the bedroom, wishing he were in that big comfortable bed, next to a certain, warm body.

Only he wasn't thinking about sleeping.

Chapter Eight

A distant ringing pierced his sleep, but he couldn't quite raise his eyelids. He hadn't gotten much rest.

Until the door to the bedroom swung open and a frantic Megan whispered, "Rick, come get in the bed!"

He snapped awake at once and leaped to his feet, pulling her against him as she reached his side, his lips covering hers.

Megan was stunned by Rick's reaction. He must not yet be awake. She pushed against him, twisting her lips away from his. "No, Rick!"

He frowned as he opened his eyes. "No? But you said—"

"The lady is bringing up our breakfast. She said to stay in bed. She'd use her key." While she explained, she was gathering up the blanket and pillow, still warm from his large body—now covered only in a pair of white briefs.

Suddenly tongue-tied, Megan backed away, clutching the bedding.

In the silence, they both heard footsteps in the hallway.

Megan found her voice again. "Grab your clothes!" and she raced for the other room. She tossed Rick's pillow onto the bed beside hers, kicked the blanket under the bed and slid into place, doubling her pillow to support her.

Rick rushed in behind her, dumping his clothes and boots on the nearest chair. Then he got in the bed with her.

"Damn! What time is it?" he muttered.

The vibrations of his voice and the warmth of his body stopped her from answering. An echo of what must've been a dream filled her head. Had she imagined him beside her during the night?

At least with the cover over him, she didn't have to stare at all of his magnificent body. Only the upper portion of his chest was exposed to view.

Which was still more skin than she wanted to deal with. Because the compulsion to touch him, to warm her hands against him, was almost more than she could control.

"Good morning!" their hostess sang out just before she entered the bedroom.

Megan sank down a little lower under the cover, so that even her shoulders didn't show.

"Uh, good morning," Rick responded, then cleared his throat again.

Megan wondered if he was getting sick. He'd cleared his throat a lot last night, too. But she had more important things to think about right now.

"I hope you two were comfortable," the lady offered, but there was a knowing grin on her face that brought color to Megan's cheeks.

Fortunately, Rick wasn't as tongue-tied as her. "Very comfortable," he assured the woman. "This is a great bed."

"Yes, it is." With a wink, she added, "It doesn't squeak. I'm sure you noticed."

"Uh, yeah," Rick agreed, while Megan wished she could hide her head under the covers.

"I'll just set the tray over here," the innkeeper said, indicating the desk that stood near the window. "And you can eat at your leisure. No need to check out for another couple of hours in case you want to rest a little longer." She winked again and excused herself.

Megan didn't move as she listened for the second door to close. She feared if she stirred, she might accidentally bump into Rick's long legs beneath the cover. And who knew what would happen then.

After a couple of minutes of absolute silence, Rick muttered, "Man, this bed is really comfortable."

The fact that he sounded drowsy, comfortable, content, was as frightening as his words were irritating. After the adrenaline rush from the phone call and subsequent events, Megan expected something a little more to the point.

"That's all you've got to say?" she demanded, sitting up and pushing back the cover.

"Well, I could add that you look really good in that nightgown," he drawled, a grin on his face.

She snatched the cover up to her chin. How could she have forgotten?

Glaring at him, her heart suddenly lurched. Not only did he look sexy, but he also looked exhausted. "I'm sorry. Was the sofa really uncomfortable?"

"Oh, yeah," he said with a sigh, letting his eyelids fall.

He said nothing else and Megan watched him, letting herself drink in the sight of him in her bed. His ex-wife must've been crazy to let this man get away. What more could a woman want?

She answered her own question. She could want honesty, honor and…and a man who loved her.

At least Rick was honest. And he seemed to be honorable. For a pretend marriage, that was all she could ask for. He was a simple man who worked hard.

And owned a tux.

She frowned. She'd intended to ask him about that last night, but other things had gotten in the way. She could understand Cal owning a tux. He'd lived in Dallas and was a wealthy man.

But Rick? Supposedly he was a rancher on a tight budget. Why would he need to own a tuxedo? And what about all that computer equipment he had? The downstairs bedroom was more than an office. It was a technology center.

It was like finding NASA's space exploration equipment at a small-town airport. Maybe Rick wasn't as simple a man as she'd thought. Maybe he was hiding something, as her ex-brother-in-law had.

She shuddered as fear built in her. She opened her mouth to ask him some questions but was halted by a soft snore.

He'd gone to sleep?

So much for thinking he wanted her. So much for fearing her scandalous nightgown would drive him crazy. So much for...

"Be grateful," she whispered to herself. She hadn't wanted to fight him off, had she? Memory of that sudden kiss when she'd awakened him filled her. She'd longed to lean into him, to surrender to the passion that filled her. But she'd been too worried about what was about to happen.

Yes, she should be grateful that he'd fallen asleep. Because it wouldn't take a lot of effort on his part to persuade her to abandon her rules. To convince her that sharing his passion wouldn't hurt anything.

To give herself up to the urges he created in her, overpowering urges that took a lot of determination to counteract.

Very carefully, she slid from beneath the covers. When he didn't move, she opened the suitcase and gathered up the new underwear and dress and tiptoed to the bathroom. She could have her shower and be properly dressed before she ate any of the breakfast.

And Rick could have some extra sleep in the

comfortable bed, to make up for the night on the sofa.

"RICK? RICK?"

A warm hand on his shoulder, as well as the soft voice, slowly roused him. He rolled over and opened one eye. "Yeah?"

"It's eleven-thirty. We need to check out at noon. If you want a shower and some breakfast, you'd better get moving. I'll wait in the other room."

Megan, dressed in the pale blue dress with small sprigs of flowers that clung to her body, as he'd imagined it would, began backing away from the bed.

"Have you eaten breakfast?" he asked, his mind catching up with his body.

"Yes. But there's plenty left for you, even if it is a little cold."

He sighed. "Why don't you carry the tray to the other room and I'll join you as soon as I shower." When she frowned, he added, "I'm not fond of eating in bed." He could've added alone, because the thought of eating his breakfast beside Megan, wearing that nightgown, might've been fun.

"Okay," she quickly agreed and picked up the tray.

As she moved toward the door, he shoved back the cover. "I'll get the door for you."

She whirled around, almost losing the contents of the tray. "No! I'll get it."

Oh, yeah. He'd forgotten he wasn't wearing any pants. Megan seemed upset about that. "Okay," he agreed, staying in place while she juggled the tray to open the door. When the door closed behind her, he relaxed once more against the pillow.

Some wedding night. His body ached, but not for the right reasons.

Shoving back the cover, he sat on the edge of the bed. He shouldn't be this tired. He had gotten some sleep on the sofa, even if it had been intermittent. And the time spent in this bed had been restful.

He was surprised he'd been able to sleep so soundly with Megan beside him. He guessed it just proved how tired he'd been. Memories of how she'd looked in that blue gown, her eyes huge, sent heat through his body.

With a chuckle, he questioned whether it was the blue of the nightgown or the fear he'd grab her that had made her eyes look big.

It didn't matter. This was the last time they'd share a bed, so he might as well forget it. A shower would help dismiss those kinds of thoughts from his mind.

A few minutes later, he appeared at the door to the sitting room, where Megan stood by the front window, her back to him.

"I think I'm presentable now. And hungry as a bear," he added as she spun around.

She didn't say anything, and she looked worried.

"Megan? Is something wrong?"

"No, of course not." She hesitated, then added, "At least I hope not."

He moved to her side. "What is it?"

"The four ladies, the ones you call the matchmakers, are here."

"They came in here?" he asked, surprised.

"Not to our room. After I took my shower, I came in here to eat so I wouldn't bother you. And I saw them arrive."

"Maybe they came to settle the bill."

"Probably. But I was worried that we didn't convince the woman that everything was…was normal."

He thought back to the few minutes the hostess had come into the bedroom. "I think we did."

"But your dress shoes were in here, by the couch."

"She'll probably think I was getting comfortable before we managed to get to the bed." In fact, if it had been a real honeymoon night, his clothes might've been scattered all over the place, and he wouldn't have cared.

Megan's cheeks heated up again. He'd never seen anyone blush as much as Megan. And he loved it.

He pulled her against him. "Don't worry so much. Even if we didn't convince her, the matchmakers will persuade her. They know the truth, even if they choose not to believe it."

"I guess you're right," she murmured.

Rick loved feeling her against him. She must like

it a little, too, because, as when they danced last night, she leaned her head against his shoulder.

Then she pulled back. "You'd better eat. We only have a few minutes before we're supposed to check out. I'll pack everything up in our new luggage while you eat."

"I put my tux in the big suitcase, along with my other things," he assured her as he started uncovering dishes on the tray. The sight of scrambled eggs, bacon, fresh fruit, distracted him.

"Do you use your tux often?"

"Not now," he said absentmindedly.

"What did you do before you bought your ranch?"

Suddenly, his senses were on alert. Why did she want to know? One of the things he liked about the people of Cactus was their acceptance of him as he was, without questions. "I lived in a city. Why?"

"It seemed odd that you would own your own tux."

"I bought it for a friend's wedding. He told me it would be better to buy my own. It was on sale, so I believed him."

"Oh, that makes sense."

A funny answer. "Yeah." It made sense as long as she didn't see the designer label. He was glad he'd already packed the tux, instead of leaving it to her. He had no intention of revealing his past to Megan.

Most especially to Megan.

SINCE MARYBELLE had worked the Thursday morning shift for Megan, and she wasn't scheduled for the weekend, Megan didn't have to worry about working again until Monday afternoon. Unless there was an emergency.

She and Rick arrived back at the ranch just a little after noon. When they went in the backdoor, Faith was still at the table with the children, feeding them lunch.

"Hi, Mom," Megan said, unable to keep a certain coolness out of her voice.

"Aunt Megan!" Torie cried, a relieved smile on her face. "I thought you weren't coming back!"

Faith said under her breath, "She's worried all morning."

Megan pulled out a chair next to Torie and gave her a hug. "Of course I came back. We're all going to live here with Rick, remember?"

"And Daisy!" Torie added.

Rick raised one eyebrow. "Where is that dog?"

Faith answered. "Jose asked if he could take Daisy with him to work the cows."

"Good. I need to go see how he's managing. I'll take the new luggage upstairs, Meg. Shall I put it in your room? Where's my things?"

Again Faith answered. "I moved all your things back upstairs, remember?"

"I just wanted to be sure."

"I moved some of your machines last night, with Celia's help, but I'm not sure I got them arranged or hooked up the way you would want," she added.

"Oh, Mom, you should've waited," Megan protested, concerned that her mother might have messed up some of Rick's fancy equipment, not to mention overexerted herself.

"Uh, it's okay," Rick said, but Megan could tell he was nervous about the results. "I'll move the rest of it this afternoon when I get in."

Then he hurried from the room, carrying the three suitcases.

"Where did you get the luggage?" Faith asked.

"It was part of the wedding gift," Megan said, knowing her voice sounded stiff.

Her mother looked at her from beneath her lashes and scooped up another bite of peas for Drew.

"Why didn't you warn me, Mom?"

"What good would it have done? You would've just worried," Faith said.

"Or been a little better prepared."

Faith shrugged her shoulders. "They asked me to keep it a secret, and I promised."

Frustrated, Megan turned to the door leading from the kitchen. Torie stopped her.

"Where are you going, Aunt Megan?"

"Upstairs, to unpack, sweetie. Finish your lunch and then I'll read you a story before you take your nap."

"A Pooh bear story?" Torie asked, her gaze filled with hope.

Who could resist? Of course, the fact that it was the longest book Torie owned probably had something to do with her request. "Yes, the Pooh bear story. But you have to eat your vegetables first."

"Okay," Torie agreed, immediately cramming a large bite of carrots into her mouth with both the spoon and her hand.

"Torie, your manners!" Faith urged.

Megan slipped from the room without Torie noticing. She climbed the stairs and stopped at the first room, Rick's.

He'd left the door open.

"Do you want me to hang up your tux so you can join Jose?" she asked.

"No, I hung it up, thanks, Megan. I, uh, I put the suitcases in your room since I emptied the big one. Or I can store them in my closet, after you finish unpacking. I have a bigger closet than you."

"All right, that would be nice. Did Mom mess up any of your equipment?" she asked, her gaze traveling over several of the machines.

"No, I'm sure she didn't. But tell her not to move the others. They're heavy. I'll take care of them when I get back to the house."

"I will. I'm sorry for all the inconvenience. I want to tell you again how much we appreciate what you've done."

He moved toward the door and she stepped aside. But he didn't pass her by. Clasping her shoulders, he leaned toward her and she thought he was going to kiss her.

"Megan, we're each doing something for the other. Remember how this house looked before you and your mother cleaned it? And all that good food you've cooked? I'm not suffering.''

"I hope not," she muttered, refusing to look at him. He was too close.

So when he did kiss her, she wasn't prepared.

Fortunately, he only brushed his lips across hers and hurried down the stairs, leaving Megan standing in his bedroom doorway, wishing things were different than they were.

RICK JOINED Jose and worked hard all afternoon, in spite of Jose's teasing about his honeymoon. He distracted his friend by teasing him right back about the young lady he'd brought to the wedding.

"Maybe you're planning on heading up the aisle, just like I did?"

"Hey, I just met the lady. Don't be rushing me. Some of us don't make decisions as fast as you do.''

"I guess I was a little quick, but I didn't want her to get away," Rick assured him, realizing he wasn't completely lying. Megan needed his help and he felt she deserved a little consideration.

"Besides," Jose added, "since I have to work for other people part of the time instead of for myself, I'm not ready to take on more responsibility."

Jose had a small place, but he supplemented his income by working for Rick three days a week. When he could, Jose intended to train horses. He had a natural ability that impressed Rick.

"Yeah, a wife and family are a big responsibility," Rick said with a sigh.

"You gonna adopt those kids?"

The question shocked Rick. Of course he wasn't, because the marriage wasn't real, but he realized if it was, that would be what he wanted. "Uh, Megan and I haven't discussed it. Things happened too quickly."

"They're cute kids."

"Yeah. And Torie is getting used to me. As long as she can play with Daisy," he added with a grin.

Rick was still thinking about Torie as he and Daisy headed back to the ranch at sunset. He figured the little girl would ask about swimming in the creek, as he'd promised, when he got to the house.

He'd told Megan he didn't mind Torie's fondness for his dog. And he didn't. As a child, he'd had a pet. Fluffy had been part cocker spaniel and part something else. She'd been a faithful companion as he'd navigated childhood. When his mother had died, Fluffy had consoled him.

Maybe he should get Torie her own puppy. Daisy was a work dog, but if Torie had her own puppy, housebroken of course, she'd have the constant companionship that had meant so much to him.

He'd ask around town, see if anyone had puppies they needed to find homes for.

And maybe he'd better talk to Megan, too. He didn't want to do anything to upset her. After all, she was the temporary legal guardian for the children.

Should he get Drew a puppy, too? The baby seemed too young yet, but Megan would know. They'd make the decision together.

Like husband and wife.

That thought occupied his mind until he got to the barn. As he unsaddled his horse, he realized they had a visitor, if the car parked beside the house was anything to go by.

And he thought he recognized the vehicle. It looked like Mac Gibbons's sport utility vehicle.

Mac Gibbons, his wife's attorney.

Had she already decided to back out of their marriage?

Chapter Nine

"Hey, Mac, how are things?" Rick asked as he entered the kitchen, trying to remain calm.

Mac, who had been seated at the table across from Megan, stood and shook his hand. "Good. How's married life?"

Rick shot a quick glance at Megan, looking for reassurance, but she kept her gaze fixed on the table, her hands clasped in front of her. Tempting fate, Rick put his hands on her shoulders and leaned over to drop a kiss on her temple.

"It's wonderful," he assured Mac.

Mac gave him a well-satisfied smile. "Yeah, it is, isn't it?"

"What brings you out here this late in the day?"

Mac looked at Megan, and she gave a faint nod. "I received a call today from Drake Moody's attorney. He's fighting the temporary custody."

Rick pulled out the chair beside Megan and covered her clasped hands with one of his. "Isn't he still in prison?"

"Yeah. He wants his parents to have custody until he's out."

"I thought Megan intended to have the custody hearing here, instead of Fort Worth." He could feel her hands trembling beneath his and wanted to wrap his arms around her.

"We've talked about that. The temporary custody order was issued in Fort Worth and that's what he wants changed, so we'll have to deal with that in Fort Worth. We've already filed for permanent custody here."

Rick nodded and waited.

Finally, Mac sighed. "We're going to need to go to Fort Worth for the hearing. Can you come with Megan?"

"Of course I can. Do we take the kids?"

"No, I don't think that will be necessary, though they may send a social worker out to check on their situation, to interview Torie, at least."

"Yeah, Drew's not much of a conversationalist," Rick said, hoping to bring some relief to Megan. "When do we go?"

"It's set for Monday morning, nine a.m."

"Okay, we can drive down on Sunday." He looked at Megan for confirmation, but she never moved.

"Or you can fly in with me early Monday morning. Whichever you choose."

Since Megan wasn't responding, which was worrying Rick, he murmured, "We'll talk it over and let you know."

"Great. Well, any questions, Megan?"

She shook her head no.

Rick stood and offered his hand, thanking Mac for coming out. Then he followed him outside.

"Okay, what has Megan so panicked?" he asked when Mac reached his vehicle.

Mac sighed. "She'd hoped to avoid facing a judge in Fort Worth. Moody apparently has some influence there."

"Yeah, she told me that. Do we have a chance?"

"Yes, but I need more to work with. Could the two of you afford a private investigator to collect information on Moody? If he's as bad as Megan says, there's got to be—"

"Hire one," Rick said at once.

"I won't charge for my services, but a P.I.—"

"Expense isn't a problem, Mac. We'll pay your bill and the P.I.'s. Just let me know how much." He paused, then added, "But don't say anything to Megan. I don't want her to worry about money."

"You're sure?"

"I'm sure."

Mac clapped him on the shoulder. "You're a good man, Rick Astin."

Rick shrugged off the praise. "You'd do the same for your wife, wouldn't you?"

"In a heartbeat," Mac agreed. "There's just one thing."

"What's that?"

"There mustn't be any hint of…if you spend

Sunday night in Fort Worth, it has to appear...you'll have to share a hotel room.''

Rick didn't know what Mac knew...and didn't want to know. But he got the message. "No problem.''

Just like last night was no problem. He'd get almost no sleep and be frustrated, but, hey, it was for the kids.

"Great. Let me know when you two are going down.''

"Will do.''

Rick stood watching Mac drive away.

He'd just broken a promise to himself. But there was more at stake here than his pride, or the game he'd been playing. Babies needed to be protected. Megan needed him. His family, even if it was temporary, depended on him.

And it felt damn good.

MEGAN STOOD at the kitchen sink, staring out the window at Mac and Rick talking. *What were they saying? Was Mac telling Rick they had no hope?*

He hadn't said that to her, but Megan feared that was what he was thinking. Had she made a mistake, running away from Fort Worth, hiring a local attorney?

Mac was good. She trusted him. But he wouldn't be on his home turf. Should she hire another attorney? And would she have enough money to see this through?

She looked outside again and realized Mac had

left and Rick was nowhere in sight. Probably he'd retreated to the barn, not even the evening meal tempting him to come back in.

The sound of boots had her spinning around to find she'd mistaken Rick's direction. She couldn't even form a welcoming smile, fear had such a hold on her.

To her surprise, he headed straight for her. When he reached her, he wrapped his arms around her and pressed her against his long form.

"It's okay, baby," he whispered, and Megan lost control completely, her body shaking like a leaf in a storm.

"N-No, it's not! We're g-going to lose them. H-He—"

"No, we're not. Those children are depending on us to keep them safe, and that's what we'll do."

She pushed back a little so she could see his face. "You don't understand. Drake Moody has money and power. Fort Worth is his territory. I thought if we came here, could get the custody battle moved here, we could—"

"And we will. The judge isn't going to move the children without a good reason. Thanks to you and your mother, they've got a good home. They're receiving loving care. There's no reason to move them."

"That's what Mac said."

"And he's right."

Some of his reason and the warmth of his body

began to invade her, warding off the chill Mac's announcement had brought her.

Faith peeked around the kitchen door. "May we come in?"

Megan jumped from Rick's hold as if she'd been doing something illegal. "Of course!"

Rick grinned at his mother-in-law. "You bet. I hope that means we're going to eat. I'm starving."

Megan watched her mother respond to those words like an army horse hearing the bugler sound the charge. She settled Drew in the high chair and immediately began to put the dinner on the table.

"I was going to feed the children earlier, but the lawyer came and—"

"Where is he?" Torie whispered, still standing by the door, as if ready for a quick escape.

"Who?" Rick asked.

"The man who made Aunt Megan cry."

Rick's gaze immediately shifted to Megan, and she wanted to hide. "Is she talking about Mac?"

"I don't like him," Torie protested.

"Sweetie, Mr. Gibbons is a nice man," Megan hurriedly assured her niece, crossing the room to pick her up.

"H-He said my daddy's name."

Megan saw the fear in her niece's gaze and shuddered. She couldn't lose this battle. She couldn't abandon Torie to her father's sadistic behavior. Or Drew, she added, staring at the baby's sweet smile as he banged on the tray of his high chair. She couldn't.

"Your daddy wanted to know if you're okay," she said, flashing a warning to her mother and Rick with her gaze.

"I don't want him to come," Torie said, her eyes filling with tears.

Megan didn't know what to say. She couldn't promise Drake would never come. She couldn't even promise to keep Torie and Drew safe. Tears gathered in her eyes, too.

Then Rick lifted Torie out of Megan's arms. She started to protest, but she realized Torie wasn't.

"Hey, you, I don't want him to come either," Rick said, but he was grinning.

"Are you 'fraid of him, too?" Torie whispered.

"Nope. I'm not afraid of him. But I don't want him to come because I like our family the way it is."

"Me, too," she said softly, one arm going around his neck.

"I had an idea today. But we need to ask your mommy—" Rick broke off, catching his mistake. "I mean, we need to ask your Aunt Megan about it."

Torie leaned forward and whispered. Megan could just barely hear her words. "Sometimes I call her Mommy, too. I don't think my real mommy cares. She went away."

Megan's heart ached at Torie's sad words. She and her sister hadn't always agreed on everything, but she'd loved her. And Andrea had loved her children.

They were the reason she'd finally left Drake. And they were the reason she left with him in his car. They were supposed to discuss the children's future.

Megan caressed Torie's blond curls. "You can call me Mommy if you like, Torie. Your real mommy won't mind and you're my little girl, now."

Torie leaned into Megan's caress. But she looked at Rick. "Does that mean you're my daddy?"

Megan gasped, unable to think of anything to say.

Rick, however, after looking surprised, nodded. "I guess I am. So, guess what I thought we should discuss with Mommy?"

"What?"

"I wondered if maybe you'd like your very own puppy?"

All the tragedy, the angst, the worry was forgotten. Torie squealed with delight, clapping her little hands together. "Yes, yes, yes!"

Megan opened her mouth to protest. But the joy on Torie's face stopped her. Even Drew, not sure what he was cheering about, clapped his pudgy hands together and squealed with his sister.

Faith had stopped putting dinner on the table, watching the three of them talk. Now she reached for Torie.

"Time for dinner, young lady. You and your brother have to get your baths and get tucked in bed soon. We'll discuss puppies tomorrow."

RICK FIGURED Faith's scolding words were aimed at him as much as Torie. But he hadn't been able to bear the heartbreaking sadness in the little girl's eyes and words.

"I want to sit by Daddy," Torie complained as Faith put her in a chair by Megan.

Both women turned to stare at the little girl, and Rick almost chuckled out loud. Hey, it wasn't his sterling personality. It was the puppy.

Megan silently switched places with Torie, putting the child between her and Rick.

The platters were passed around and Rick tucked into another well-cooked meal. Chicken-fried steak tonight, with creamed potatoes, pinto beans and a tossed salad.

"How big is a puppy?" Torie whispered, leaning toward him.

Rick looked up and found Megan's gaze on him, as well as Torie's. "I don't know. I'll look for a puppy tomorrow. And you can be thinking of a name."

The rest of the meal, Torie tried out various names on her audience. Megan shot a glare at Rick after the thirtieth name was discussed ad nauseam. "Torie, eat your dinner. It's almost your bedtime."

Just as Faith was picking up Drew to take both children upstairs for their baths, Torie had another question.

"What about Drew? Does he get a puppy, too?"

"No!" Megan exclaimed without waiting for Rick's answer.

He grinned. "No, honey, one puppy will be enough. You'll get to name the puppy, but you have to share it with Drew."

"Okay, I'll share," Torie promised. Then she raced around the table to take Faith's hand.

Megan, who had promised to do the dishes if Faith took care of the baths, stood and began clearing the table. Rick rose and picked up several dirty plates.

"I'll do it," Megan said sharply.

"I'll help," he said firmly, not willing to be shut out. Megan seemed to think they could keep strict lines in this situation. He didn't.

"That's not your job, Rick."

He leaned over and kissed her as he walked past. Just a brief kiss, not what he wanted. But enough to get her attention. "*Our* job is to keep those babies happy and safe. I'm doing my part."

"Was that the reason for the puppy?"

"Yeah. And it worked. Torie forgot all about her father."

"I wish I could," Megan confessed, slumping against the kitchen cabinet.

Rick set down the dirty plates and took her in his arms again. He knew how he'd like to distract her, but he couldn't take advantage of her emotions.

"Maybe I should get you a puppy, too," he suggested, a warm smile in place when she pushed back and stared at him. To his relief, a gurgle of laughter escaped her.

"Maybe helping with the dishes is a better idea," she told him, still smiling.

He couldn't resist. Planting a smacking kiss on her soft lips, he released her. "Your wish is my command, Mrs. Astin."

Turning back to the table, he began clearing it again, thinking he was fortunate Megan didn't realize how much he'd meant those words.

AFTER THE kitchen was cleaned, Rick went to his bedroom. He still needed to move the rest of his equipment, but first he had some phone calls to make.

The fourth call did the trick. Herk Jones, one of his neighbors, had six puppies, yellow lab and retriever mix, that were ready for new homes.

Rick returned to the kitchen. Faith and Megan were sitting at the kitchen table, tightly holding hands, quietly talking.

"Am I interrupting?" he asked, pausing by the door.

Faith managed a smile. "No. Megan was explaining what Mac had to say, but she's finished."

Rick gave his mother-in-law an encouraging smile. "Things are going to go our way, Faith. We're going to protect the kids."

"I hope you're right."

"I am. The biggest thing you've got to worry about is training a puppy." He grinned and added, "Sorry, I know I kind of sprang the idea on you, but I couldn't stand for Torie to look so sad."

Faith stood and walked over and, much to Rick's surprise, stood on her tiptoes and kissed his cheek. "You've got a good heart, Rick. I can handle a puppy if it means Torie is happy."

"Good, 'cause we can pick it up tomorrow."

With a faint smile, Faith patted Rick's arm. "Then I'd better get to bed. I'll need my rest." She walked to the door, but her gaze was fixed on her daughter, an anxious look on her face.

"Go on," Rick said softly. "I think Megan wants to discuss names for the dog with me."

Megan's head snapped up and she glared at Rick. "I certainly do not. Torie took care of that problem at dinner."

"I suppose we could leave it up to her," Rick said slowly, as if considering her words. He winked at Faith and she nodded to him before calling out a good-night and leaving the room.

Rick crossed to the table. "Come on, gloomy Gus, I want to show you something."

"This is no joke, Rick!" Megan snapped. "We could lose the kids!"

He pulled her to her feet. "I know that, Megan," he assured her, wiping any amusement from his face. "But we're not going to. And whatever happens, getting depressed about it isn't going to help anything."

She bowed her head.

Wrapping an arm around her, he pulled her up and led her to the back porch where a porch swing hung. He hadn't spent much time in the porch swing since he bought the place. It had felt too lonely to sit there at night by himself.

He sat them both down in the swing, his arm still around Megan. After a moment of sitting stiff as a toy soldier, Megan sighed and rested her head on his shoulder. Rick pushed the swing into motion with his foot.

"I'm sorry," she finally whispered.

"For what?"

"For acting like a baby. For making you work so hard at our agreement. It would've been better for you if you'd hired a housekeeper instead of putting up with our problems."

Instead of responding directly to her remarks, Rick continued to push the swing. Then he said, "You know, no one has ever called me daddy before."

"I'm sorry. I'll tell Torie not to—"

"You'll do no such thing. I'm not complaining. I kind of liked it."

"But you don't want a family. You said you'd never marry again."

Rick chuckled. "I said I didn't want a wife. Not a real one. But a family? I always thought it would be neat to have a couple of kids."

Megan sighed. "Life is so complicated."

"Yeah, but it can be pretty great, too. Look up there," he directed, pointed up to the velvet blue night. A silver-dollar moon shone down on them. "That's what I wanted to show you."

"It's lovely. Everything is lovely here. So quiet and peaceful. So safe."

"And we're going to keep it that way. You just keep believing, sweetheart. That's all it takes." He kissed her forehead.

"Rick, I…it's not fair to you."

"What's not fair?"

"You're giving so much."

"You think I should renegotiate our deal? Maybe I could ask you to sleep with me on alternate Thursdays?"

She gasped.

Rick chuckled. "Don't get upset. I'm teasing."

"But—"

"Megan, *if* we share a bed, it will be because we both choose to do so for ourselves. And no other reason. Understand?"

"Yes," she said with a sigh, her head still resting on his shoulder.

Rick knew how to take her attention off her problems. "And I just want to tell you I'm ready whenever you are."

She leaped up from the swing.

Chapter Ten

Damn, he'd done a good job.

His first breakfast at home as a married man was a silent one. Neither Faith nor the children were up yet. To his surprise, Megan was in the kitchen when he got downstairs a little after six.

But after his remark last night, Megan wouldn't look at him or speak to him. She fed him, but that was all.

"Do you work today?" he finally asked.

"No."

"When would be a good time to take Torie to pick out her puppy?" He polished off the bacon and eggs, sopping up the last of the eggs with his biscuit. She still hadn't answered when he finished. "Come on, Meg, quit treating me like a criminal. It's not against the law to tell you that I want you."

"That wasn't part of the agreement."

"Hey, I know that, or I'd be a lot more content right now."

She squared around, her fists cocked on her trim hips. "How do you know? I might be lousy at sex."

The significance of her words almost passed by him as he enjoyed her challenge. Then he stared at her, horror on his face. "You're a virgin?"

"I didn't say that," she snapped and whirled around, turning her back to him.

He ignored those words. "Why?"

"Why what?" she asked as she furiously scrubbed at an already clean sink.

He stood and carried his dirty dishes to the sink, but he was careful not to touch her. "Why haven't you ever, uh, you know, been with a man?"

"You think no one ever asked?" she challenged.

"Not likely," he assured her. "You've had *me* drooling ever since we met."

She turned bright red and looked away. "That's none of your business."

Rick wondered who would be more involved than her husband. But he wasn't really her husband, and he'd made it clear that he didn't want to be. So she was right.

He backed away. "Uh, I'll start my day. How about right before lunch?"

She gave him a puzzled look.

"To go get the dog. I figured Torie took a nap after lunch."

"Okay, fine. I'll have her ready."

He panicked. "You're coming with us, aren't you? I mean, I like Torie, but I don't know how to take care of her by myself."

For the first time since he'd entered the kitchen,

Megan smiled. "One of us will go with you, I promise."

"Okay. I have to run into town for a little while, but I'll be back by eleven."

MEGAN SANK back against the counter and let out a big sigh when Rick left the kitchen.

She was in trouble.

The man was being an angel, a protective, thoughtful angel. She couldn't ask for more to protect her niece and nephew. When they'd made their arrangement, she'd figured a marriage certificate, a man as a figurehead, was what she'd get.

Rick had given her so much more.

He'd comforted, consoled, teased. He'd reached out to Torie. The child had even called him daddy, though Megan didn't intend to encourage that.

But last night he'd indicated he wanted more. Oh, he'd said he was teasing, but it had always been Megan's theory that teasing had an element of truth in it.

The scary part was it would be so easy to give herself to him. He was sexy, kind, honest. He was protecting the children.

And there was something in her that lit up like a firecracker when he touched her.

She straightened, stiffening her shoulders. So okay, she'd have to avoid his touch. She could do that. She'd stay focused on the problem at hand. Once she got custody of the children, then she'd deal with Rick.

An annulment would be a lot simpler than a divorce.

Drew's fussing interrupted her thoughts. The baby monitor on the cabinet told her her nephew was ready for his breakfast.

She hurried upstairs to him before he woke his sister. Torie usually slept until eight, another hour and a half away. Megan didn't want her tired if they were going to pick out her puppy today.

With Drew in his high chair, Megan began the rest of her day, distracted from the thoughts that had interrupted her sleep the night before.

RICK HEADED INTO town around eight-thirty. He'd decided he needed to consult with Mac in more detail.

When he reached the town square, where Mac, and Tuck's wife, Alex, had their offices, he discovered Mac's office didn't open until nine o'clock. He changed direction and headed for the sheriff's office.

Cal, sitting with his feet propped up enjoying a cup of coffee in his office, saw Rick as he entered. "Hey, bridegroom, grab a cup of coffee and come join me."

Rick did as he suggested, snagging a doughnut, too. After all, breakfast had been a couple of hours ago.

"How's married life?" Cal asked.

"Great, except I'm tired of answering that question," Rick told him, recalling Mac's same question the night before.

"Ah. Life under the microscope. Well, that's life in a small town. Get used to it," Cal suggested with a huge grin.

"I will, but it'd be easier if the matchmakers didn't help."

Cal's grin widened even more. "Aw, come on, they were doing you a favor. A night of bliss with your new bride."

Rick rolled his eyes. "That's not why I'm here." He didn't want to discuss his marriage with anyone.

"Something wrong?" Cal was suddenly all business.

"Not yet. I'm actually in town to see Mac. He came out last night to tell us we have to be in court in Fort Worth on Monday. Megan's brother-in-law is challenging the temporary guardianship."

"What does Mac think?"

"He said he thought we'd be okay. But Megan is worried."

"Yeah." There was a wealth of understanding in that one word.

"I wondered what you knew about the man."

"Moody? Mac asked me the same question. I pulled everything I could off the computer and gave it to him."

Rick sighed and sipped the hot coffee. "Megan hasn't said much. How bad a character is he?"

"I don't know. Megan talked to Mac, but the only things on his record are a couple of DWIs."

"That's not a lot to cut him off from his kids." Rick couldn't help thinking if someone tried to take his kids from him, he'd do whatever it took to get them back. Then it occurred to him that he was beginning to feel the same way about Torie and Drew.

"Megan told Samantha he was abusive," Cal said thoughtfully, frowning, "but I don't know what that entailed."

Rick raised his eyebrow. "And Dr. Gibbons told you?"

Cal grinned. "She didn't tell Samantha as a patient. And Samantha told Mac. After all, he's her husband."

"And he told you because you're the sheriff?" Rick deduced.

"He wanted me to know what to look for in the records."

"Okay, I'll see if Mac is in yet."

"Want me to go with you?"

"You're not busy here?"

"Naw. And I'll tell 'em where to find me if something comes up."

After making arrangements, the two men walked to Mac's office to find him just settling in to the day's business. They covered Drake Moody's record quickly, and Mac said he'd hired the best P.I. he knew in Fort Worth to see what else he could find.

Rick leaned forward. "Okay, here's what I want to know. Should I call in some markers? I know a few influential people in Fort Worth."

"You do?" Mac asked with a frown. "Like who?"

Rick ran down a mental list. "The mayor, a couple of councillors, some businessmen."

Cal spoke up. "This judge granted the temporary custody to Megan originally, didn't he? So he must not favor Moody."

Mac shook his head. "When it came up after her sister's death, Megan said Moody and his family were involved in saving his skin. They all ignored the children."

"And since then?" Rick asked.

"They've ignored the children," Mac repeated with a nod.

"They haven't seen them since her sister died?" Rick asked, wanting to be sure he understood.

"They haven't even called. They didn't attend the funeral. Nothing."

"Won't that count against them?"

"Yeah, if we've got a fair judge." Mac blew out a suppressed breath.

"Give me his name and I'll see what I can do," Rick said.

"Rick, I can't be a party to bribery or—"

Grinning, Rick reassured Mac. "I'm not going to do anything illegal. I'm just going to let some people know I'll be there, and make sure there'll be some attention paid to what happens."

Mac gave him the name.

"Can I use the phone here? I don't want to make the calls from the house."

Mac offered him Alex's office. She wasn't in this morning.

After Rick left the room, Cal looked at Mac. "Will that do any good?"

"Depends on how interested those people will be in Rick's business. What did he do before he came here?"

"He's never said. I assumed he worked on a ranch. He's pretty knowledgeable."

"I know he grew up on a farm, but—he did have a tux for the wedding."

Cal frowned. "Damn. I'm supposed to be the observant one. That would be unusual for a cowboy, wouldn't it?"

Mac nodded.

"Maybe I should've done a little investigating about him, but he's a friend now. I'd feel funny looking into his background."

"Yeah."

As they sat there, thinking about the situation, the door opened and Rick reappeared.

"Did you do any good?" Mac asked.

"Maybe. The mayor plans to be in the courtroom Monday. He knows the Moody family. Doesn't care for them much. Said he'd make sure the press picked up on it."

"Good." Mac didn't say anything else, but he looked worried.

"What?" Rick asked.

"Damn, it's awkward to ask, but...but why would the mayor care?"

Rick slumped down in the nearest chair, his lips pressed tightly together. He'd known the time would come when he had to reveal his past. But he'd been enjoying his anonymity.

Finally, he lifted his head and stared at Mac. "Have you ever heard of CAP Computers?"

Cal frowned, but Mac nodded at once. "Of course. It's a major computer company out of Austin. The guy who started it sold it last year for a few billion," he said, grinning.

"Yeah." Rick didn't say anything else.

Cal and Mac stared at him. Finally, Cal said, "That was you?"

He nodded.

"Damn, man, what are you doing chasing ornery cows?" Cal demanded.

"I could ask you the same question, Cal. You've got a job. I know the oil money your family has makes working unnecessary. And you, too, Mac."

Both men nodded.

Rick pulled out his billfold and extracted a business card. Handing it to Mac, he said, "Send any bills to this man. They'll be paid." Before Mac could respond, Rick continued, "I need both of you to keep quiet about this. Even to your wives. I don't want anyone to know."

"What about Megan? Does she know?"

Rick shook his head, his lips pressed tightly together. "No. And it's important she doesn't find out."

MEGAN HAD Torie dressed in tiny blue jeans, a pink T-shirt and sneakers, her blond hair in a ponytail, bobbing with every movement.

"Where are we going?" the child asked.

"Rick is going to take us for a ride," Megan explained for the tenth time.

"When?"

"He should be here any minute," Megan said again. "Why don't you go watch cartoons? I'll call you when he gets here."

"I'm hungry."

Megan sighed. "Okay, get in your chair. You can have two cookies and a glass of milk. But that's all."

Torie chuckled. "You sound just like Mom—" She stopped, confusion and sadness in her gaze. "Why did Mommy go away?"

Megan poured the milk and carried it to the table with a plate of cookies before she answered. "Mommy died, Torie. Remember, we talked about it? She's in heaven with the angels. She'd come back if she could because she loved you very much."

"Did she love Drew?"

"Of course she did."

"Did she love Daddy?"

Tricky question. "She did, once. But Daddy… changed. He was mean to you. Mommy didn't like that. Remember? That's why you all moved in with Grandma."

"I 'member. I was glad."

"Eat your cookies, sweetie. I think I hear Rick coming."

After taking a bite, Torie asked, "Will I like it?"

"Don't talk with your mouth full. Will you like what?"

"Where we're going?"

"Yes, I think you will."

To Megan's relief, the backdoor opened and Rick walked in.

"Morning, ladies."

Torie giggled. "I'm not a lady."

"Yes, you are. You're a special lady 'cause you've got cookies." He leaned close and pretended to take a bite of Torie's cookie. She shrieked and pressed her half-eaten cookies against her chest.

Megan laughed at their playing. "There's more cookies for you, Rick." Without waiting for his approval, she placed several on a plate for him.

"Thanks, but we've got to get moving. I've got a lot of work to do this afternoon."

"Have you been in town all morning?" she asked, wondering what had been so important. When he looked at her as if she was prying, she hurried to say, "I just wondered."

"Yeah."

His terse response didn't encourage any further questions. Fine. If he wanted to have secrets, he could. She didn't care. Much.

"Ready, Torie?" Rick asked, taking two cookies in his hand and standing.

"Yep, I'm ready. What for?"

Rick knelt beside the little girl's chair, pulling it from the table so she could get down. "Ready to go get your puppy."

There was no holding Torie still after that. She threw her arms around Rick's neck as she slid from the chair, almost knocking him over. After squeezing his neck tightly, she broke loose and ran around the room, repeating "Puppy! Puppy!" over and over again.

Before Megan could corral her, she suddenly darted to the kitchen door and ran up the stairs. "Grandma! Grandma! I'm going to get a puppy."

"Torie!" Megan called, hurrying up after her.

Before she could catch Torie, she heard Drew's cry. She was too late. Torie had awakened her brother from his morning nap.

Megan calmed the little boy and came down a couple of minutes later, carrying Drew, Torie close behind. "Sorry to keep you waiting."

"I suspect it's my fault. I didn't know she'd get so excited. Are we taking Drew, too?"

"If you don't mind. Mom can fix lunch and have it ready when we get back. With Drew up, it would be harder to do."

"Okay, let's go."

A HALF HOUR later, Megan discovered just how patient Rick could be.

Torie had clapped her hands and hugged every puppy at the Jones ranch several times. The puppies, delighted with a new playmate, had jumped up and licked her face over and over again.

Still, Torie hadn't made her selection.

"Sweetie, you have to choose which puppy you want to take home," Megan urged. "We can't take any more of Mr. Jones's time."

Torie giggled as another puppy licked her. But she proved she'd heard her aunt. Putting a finger to her rosebud lips, she said, "I want flower."

Rick squatted down. "Flower?"

"That one," Torie said, pointing to the smallest puppy.

"That's the runt of the litter," Herk Jones warned.

"He looks healthy," Rick ventured.

"*She* is. But she won't get as big as the others. Won't make a good huntin' dog."

"Perfect," Rick assured the man. "The dog is a pet for Torie."

"Well, I reckon the runt won't cost as much," the older man said, rubbing his chin.

Megan jerked her head up. *Rick was paying for the dog?* She'd assumed Mr. Jones was giving them the puppy.

She couldn't see how much Rick paid the man, so she made a note to ask him later.

Torie gathered the puppy she'd chosen, squeezing it against her chest. Even though it was the smallest puppy, it was almost too big for the little girl to carry.

Rick bent down and scooped girl and dog into his arms. "Ready?"

"Yes, Flower and me are ready. Thank you, Mr. Man," she said over her shoulders to Mr. Jones.

The man grinned and waved them off.

Once both children were buckled into their seats, with the trembling puppy sitting between them, they set off for home.

Megan couldn't help smiling at the antics of the puppy and the two children in the backseat. Drew was as enthusiastic as Torie, stretching in his carseat to reach the dog.

"Thank you so much," she murmured to the man beside her.

"It will keep her busy while we're gone Monday. I told Mac to make us reservations with his for the flight early Monday morning."

Megan's smile disappeared. "You talked to Mac?"

"Yeah."

"When?"

He gave her a cautious look. "While I was in town this morning."

"Did you discuss the—the situation with him?" Her insides were churning.

"A little. I had a couple of questions."

"You had no business doing that. Mac is *my* attorney, and he shouldn't have discussed it with you." She'd watched her sister's husband take control over her life. Nothing Andrea did had remained in her control. Megan wouldn't allow that to happen to her.

"Calm down, Megan. He didn't reveal anything much."

"I will make the decisions about this case, Rick. It has nothing to do with you."

"I think it does. I'm your husband."

"No, you're not! And you don't make the decisions. I do! I'll decide if we're flying to Dallas!" She knew she was out of control, but fear boiled up in her.

"Okay, but if we drive, you'll have to share a bed with me, because I'm not sleeping on any damned couch this time."

Chapter Eleven

Saturday Megan apologized.

She served the crow along with breakfast, the one time of the day when she and Rick were alone. "I lost control. I panicked, and I'm sorry."

"What caused you to panic?" he asked.

"My...my sister's husband took over her life. She wasn't allowed to make even the smallest decision. He'd contradict her even if it wasn't what he wanted. I have to make the decisions. You've been wonderful, but if things go wrong—"

"Fair enough," Rick agreed. "I wasn't trying to take over, but I guess it was a little insensitive of me to talk to Mac without your knowledge."

"Thank you," she murmured, feeling he'd been more than generous. "I'd like us to fly with Mac Monday morning, if you don't mind. I'll arrange for the tickets."

"I never told Mac to change the arrangements. He said he'd take care of the tickets and bill us. So don't worry about it." He paused, then added softly, "Unless you want to contradict me just to prove me wrong."

Her head snapped up, realizing he was repeating her words about Drake. Was she doing that?

A shudder shook her. "No. No, I don't want to do that. Thank you for making the arrangements."

He nodded and continued to eat as if they hadn't argued.

She'd prepared a special breakfast, making pancakes, frying bacon and cutting up fresh fruit. As she'd learned early on, the way to Rick's heart, or forgiveness, was through his stomach.

"Good breakfast," he said, wiping his face with his napkin.

"Would you like more? I can fix—"

"No," he assured her with a smile. "I won't be able to get on a horse if I eat any more."

He shoved himself back from the table.

"Um, I'm going in to work this morning," she said quickly.

"I thought you were off until Monday?"

"I was, but I need Marybelle to work for me because of the trip to Fort Worth. So I traded with her."

"Okay, will your mother be okay with the kids?"

"With the kids and Flower?" she added with a wry smile.

"Oh, yeah. How's Flower doing?"

A little yip outside the kitchen door was his answer.

Megan crossed over and opened the door for the puppy. While she had quickly learned her way to the kitchen, the pup hadn't quite learned to push her way through the door.

"I've got to let her out at once. We're working on the housebreaking, but—" Megan stopped because Flower was demonstrating her lack of training on the kitchen floor.

"Damn," Rick muttered. "I'll get the mop."

THEIR FLIGHT left at six-ten Monday morning. Megan got up at four-thirty to give herself plenty of time to make sure she looked as professional as possible.

It suddenly occurred to her that she hadn't discussed Rick's appearance with him. Would he have a suit? When they went to church yesterday, he'd worn pressed jeans, a shirt and a tweed sport coat, standard attire in Cactus.

And it would be just fine, she assured herself. Rick was a good, honest man, unlike her brother-in-law. Whatever he wore would be fine.

That determined decision made his appearance all the more of a shock.

When he came to the kitchen at five, she was pouring two glasses of orange juice. Fortunately she hadn't yet picked them up to carry them to the table.

Standing before her was Rick, looking like the perfect cover model for *GQ* magazine. A navy pinstriped suit, a red and blue silk tie, a crisp white shirt, a gold watch that looked like—a Rolex.

"You have a Rolex?" she blurted out.

He looked at his watch in surprise. "Er, yeah. It was a gift."

She immediately decided it had been a gift from his wife. And she hated it! She was so preoccupied with his watch that it was several minutes after they sat down to eat the breakfast she'd prepared that she remembered the rest of his appearance.

"That's a nice suit. You look very...very sophisticated."

"Thanks. So do you."

She blushed. She'd tried to look as professional as possible. But her best suit was the one she'd worn at the wedding, and she felt sure Rick had recognized it.

He said nothing else, however, concentrating on his food.

She shouldn't have been surprised. Food was important to him. She managed a few bites, but she found the coming events of the day too distracting to eat more.

"We'd better go soon. Hurry and eat."

"I'm finished."

"Meg, you didn't eat enough to feed a bird."

"I can't," she insisted, carrying her plate to the sink.

He followed her. As he put his plate in the sink, Megan reached over to brush a biscuit crumb from his suit.

"That was very wifely," he told her with a smile.

It was the nicest conversation they'd shared since their argument. But it made her nervous. "I didn't mean—"

"I'm teasing. Let's go."

The ride to the airport was silent. Megan's mind remained focused on the children and how things would turn out.

They picked up Mac at his office and drove to the small airport nearby. Soon they were in the air. Mac and Rick kept up a running conversation, but Megan only grew more and more nervous.

When Rick reached out and took her hand, giving it a warm squeeze, she should've told him she could manage without his help. Instead, she held on for dear life, finding the contact helpful in keeping her courage up.

After they reached Fort Worth, Mac picked up the rental car and the three of them drove to the courthouse.

"How long will we have to wait?" Megan whispered.

"We have about half an hour before we're to appear in court," Mac said, consulting his watch.

"There are a lot of people around," Megan said with a frown.

Rick quickly said, "Mac, why don't you take Megan on in. I've got a phone call to make."

Megan watched as the two men seemed to be communicating something, but she wasn't sure what. Mac took her arm and led her into the court-room without any more conversation.

Just as they entered, there seemed to be a con-certed rush of people behind them, but the door closed before she could be sure. "Is something ex-citing going on out there? Should we have a look?" she asked.

"Best not. We wouldn't want to get hung up on something and not be on time. The judge would frown on that." Mac ushered her to a front pew. "Besides, I want to go over a few questions again before we start."

Since nothing mattered more than the children, Megan immediately cooperated. Who cared what was happening outside? Only the children mattered.

RICK ANSWERED the reporters' questions patiently. When he'd dropped out of sight a year ago, there had been speculation about his plans, but interest had died down. Now that he'd surfaced, the re-porters wanted to know where he'd been.

He steered the conversation to the hearing, ex-plaining his concern, in subtle ways, hoping to keep their interest on the events to take place.

The reporters had done their homework and knew the basic facts about the case. Rick encour-aged them to report the verdict and interview the judge. When an older couple approached the court-room, accompanied by a man who was obviously their attorney, he pointed out the probability that they were the Moodys.

He remained outside the courtroom until almost nine o'clock. If he went in early, some of the reporters might follow him and ask questions in front of Megan.

While he wanted to do everything he could to help the children remain with Megan, he didn't want her to know of his wealth. His ex-wife, impatient with his long work hours and insufficient income, though it was certainly more than the average family, had left him for a wealthier man.

Once he'd sold the company for the phenomenal amount printed in all the papers, she'd dumped her new love and come running back to him. Cupboard love, his mother would've said. He wanted none of it.

And he didn't want Megan to know about his wealth. After their annulment, he'd explain. But not before.

He watched the Moodys, clearly distressed by all the attention their case was receiving. Rick cynically wondered if that was because they were private people, or because they feared it would affect the outcome.

When the mayor appeared, a few minutes later, Mr. Moody stepped forward to be greeted. The mayor offered him a curt nod and continued on to Rick, welcoming him with a smile.

"Rick, it's good to see you again. I'd like to take you to lunch after the hearing. There are several wonderful opportunities you might be interested in."

"Thank you, Mayor, but I've got to get back as soon as possible. My wife doesn't like to leave the children any longer than necessary."

"Yes, yes, a dedicated mother. How wonderful. But I'd hoped—"

"Why don't I have my business manager give you a call? If he thinks they're good opportunities, then I'll schedule another visit." He didn't want to start another company, but he'd missed some of the aspects of business. He might consider running something from a distance.

And he wanted to keep the mayor on his side.

"It's almost nine. I'd better join my wife and attorney. Thanks for coming, sir."

"My pleasure. We want to serve our citizens well."

Several reporters crowded around, and Rick was able to slip away. When he joined Megan and Mac, he nodded briefly to Mac, hoping to convey the news that everything was going as planned. Just before the court clerk asked everyone to rise, the Moodys and their attorney, the Mayor, and the reporters entered the courtroom.

"I think we should take our places up front," Mac said hurriedly and led Megan and Rick to one of the tables on the other side of the bar.

"There are the Moodys," Megan whispered, and Rick took her hand in his.

Frankly, he didn't see how any man in good conscience could choose such stiff, cold people over

Megan for anything, much less the care of two small children. But maybe he was prejudiced.

The judge entered the courtroom and settled into his chair before he looked up. He stared as he noted the crowded courtroom. With a dip of his head he acknowledged the presence of the mayor and the reporters before shooting what appeared to Rick to be a panicked look toward the Moodys.

Megan had been right to be worried. Rick suspected the man had intended to run roughshod over Megan and rule in the Moodys' favor without much consideration for the children's interests.

He'd figured the only thing that would stop him would be publicity over a biased decision. After all, he had to run for reelection. And if he wasn't fair, his opponent would receive a hell of a campaign contribution to help him win.

Mac was smooth in his presentation, stressing the mental health of the children, and the temporary nature of the custody, not hinting at the permanent custody request he'd already filed for his clients in west Texas. Then he put Megan on the stand and questioned her about the welfare of the children.

Though she was nervous, Rick was proud of how well she handled herself. Rick also took the stand to assure the judge he loved the children also. As he prepared to leave the witness chair, the Moodys' attorney questioned him sharply about their recent marriage.

After Rick answered briefly and in an unconcerned manner, the man then presented the

Moodys' case. When he put the Moodys, first the husband, then the wife, on the witness stand to request their grandchildren, Mac pointed out their lack of concern for the children both before and after Andrea's death.

Several of the reporters muttered when Mrs. Moody admitted she'd never even called her grandchildren. Mac asked the woman questions about Torie, but she couldn't give any particulars about her. She couldn't even give Drew's exact birth date.

There was a stirring in the courtroom as several reporters made notes. The mayor cleared his throat, and the judge looked nervous.

Rick squeezed Megan's hand.

Finally, the judge ruled in Megan's favor, stating that he saw no reason to overturn the ruling of temporary custody, though he would order a visit from social services before the ruling was final.

"But Frank, you promised—" Mr. Moody protested, standing. His lawyer dragged him down into his seat before he could finish his statement.

The judge hurriedly rapped his gavel and left the courtroom. The reporters edged forward, wanting to question Mr. Moody on what exactly the judge had promised.

Mac and Rick, with Megan between them, slipped out the side door and hurried to their rental car.

"We won!" Megan enthused after they got in. "I can't believe it. We won!"

"Hey, you had a good attorney," Rick said.

"Those reporters didn't hurt, either," Mac said dryly, shooting a glance Rick's way.

"Why were they there?" Megan asked, frowning. "This case wasn't important—"

"I think it's an election year. They were probably investigating the judge," Rick suggested.

"Well, I'm grateful, whatever the reason." She slumped against the backseat. "I'm so relieved!"

"How about we grab an early lunch and then catch the next flight out?" Mac suggested.

"Oh, yes," Megan agreed. "I'm suddenly starving. Oh, and I need to call Mom as soon as we find a phone."

Mac reached into his pocket. "Here, use my cell phone."

Megan did so. By the time she'd talked to Faith, Mac had pulled into a famous Tex-mex restaurant in Fort Worth.

During their quick lunch, Rick was relieved to have the true Megan back, the one who smiled and teased and made his heart beat faster.

On the plane home, she insisted she didn't need him to hold her hand. But as soon as the plane got in the air, she fell asleep, and her head slipped to Rick's shoulder.

Mac, seated on the other side of her, waited a couple of minutes before asking, "When are you going to tell her?"

"About what?"

"About your background."

"Never if I can manage it. It doesn't affect her."

Mac raised one eyebrow, a silent comment.

"You know the truth about our marriage, Mac, whether you want to admit it or not. We have an agreement. That's all it is. When it's over, then we'll part company."

"Uh-huh," Mac muttered, disbelief obvious.

Rick said nothing else. He wasn't sure he believed his words either. He'd been married less than a week, and he already felt that Megan, Faith and the children were his family.

Was it because he had no family now? His mother had died when he was young and his father had passed away three years ago.

He was supposed to stay married to Megan for at least six months after the permanent custody was granted. That meant close to a year sharing his life with the woman beside him.

Could he walk away? But if he couldn't, it was even more important that Megan not know about his wealth. He didn't want to be fooled a second time. He didn't want to be wanted because he had a lot of money.

He leaned his head back and closed his eyes, feeling Megan's warmth against him, smelling the floral perfume she wore, wishing, for a few moments at least, to forget the questions about the future and enjoy the present.

MEGAN SPENT the evening with the children, playing with and entertaining them, giving her mother some time to herself since she'd had them all day.

Shortly before Drew's bedtime bottle, Rick joined them, holding the little boy, also taking turns with Torie rolling a tennis ball for Flower. Then he read Torie her bedtime story while Megan gave Drew his bottle.

"Thank you for helping," she said, feeling almost shy. "You'd already worked hard moving all your equipment this afternoon."

"'Bout time I got your mother's room cleaned out. She's been very patient."

"Did you have any trouble hooking it all up again?"

"Nope."

She frowned but he said nothing else. Maybe he was really good with electronics. That certainly wasn't an area of expertise for her. She could use a computer, but she knew nothing about how it worked.

"I think I'll go on to bed," she said when he turned on the television in the living room. "It's been a long day."

"Yeah. And congratulations."

"Thanks." She went up the stairs, thinking about his warm smile. About his support. His kindness. She was ashamed to admit that she was glad today's ruling was for temporary custody, not permanent custody, because that would mean the end to their marriage.

That was a horrifying thought.

But Rick was becoming as important to her as the air she breathed. He didn't always do what she thought she wanted him to do. But he did what he thought best. And he was usually right. When they argued, he allowed her her point of view.

Which proved he wasn't like Drake.

And when he touched her, she could scarcely think of anything else, even the children.

Sharing the house with him for the next six months was going to be very difficult. Unless she gave in to what she now realized she wanted.

She'd never met a man she wanted to surrender to. A man she could trust, respect. A man she believed was honest. But now, she'd found Rick. She was eager to experience the oneness that came from the ultimate sharing.

She closed the door to her bedroom, as if to physically remind her that she mustn't cross that line. She'd only known the man a short time. She'd be foolish to even think of making that monumental a decision now.

But darn it, it was hard.

AFTER WORKING the morning shift at the clinic with Samantha, receiving her congratulations on Monday's success, Megan returned home for a late lunch. She and her mother put both children down for a nap.

Then Faith drove into town to meet Florence Greenfield for a shopping trip to Muleshoe. Florence had heard of a great sale in the nearby town.

Still feeling warm and grateful to Rick, Megan decided to spend the afternoon baking. Her first project was a German chocolate cake. When she had it in the oven, she mixed a large batch of oat-meal-raisin cookies. The kids loved those.

Then she started on the icing, the most important part of the cake.

A knock on the front door interrupted her, causing Megan to stare in that direction. No one in Cactus used the front door.

Wiping her hands on the apron she wore over her jeans and T-shirt, she hurried through the house to the front door, followed closely by Flower.

Through the glass she saw a beautiful, sophisticated woman, obviously not a resident of Cactus.

She pulled open the door and greeted the woman.

Instead of returning her greeting, the woman stepped over the threshhold and said, "Please tell Rick I'm here. I'm sure he's expecting me."

Megan had had breakfast with Rick that morning and he hadn't mentioned expecting anyone to come, especially not someone like this woman, dressed in what appeared to be a designer suit, several large diamond rings and a handbag that Megan knew cost as much as their grocery bill for a month.

"Rick's working. Perhaps he could call you this evening."

The woman looked down her nose at Megan. "I don't believe it's the housekeeper's business to make that decision."

Megan considered several answers. Finally, she chose the most polite one, though it took a lot of effort. "Who may I say is calling?"

With a haughty look, the woman said, "His wife, of course."

Chapter Twelve

It felt good to be in the saddle again.

Yesterday reminded Rick why he'd left the business world to be a rancher. Of course, he used his truck, and a lot of other modern equipment, but there was a timelessness to a man and his horse and dog, working to make a living.

Jose shouted and Rick urged his mount in that direction. A cow was in distress, the birthing not coming easy.

"I think we'll have to pull it," Jose said, already dismounted.

Rick did the same, leaving the reins trailing the ground, knowing his horse was trained to stay in place. "Yeah. Well, let's see what we can do to help this little mama."

Half an hour later, both men were hot and sweaty and covered in blood and other sundry fluids, but they were congratulating each other on their success, when Rick's cell phone rang.

He'd started carrying it when Megan and her family had moved in, telling her to call him if there was an emergency. He hurried to his horse and dug the cell phone out of his saddlebag.

"Meg? What's wrong?"

There was static and he strode a few paces over to higher ground. "What did you say? I couldn't hear you."

"*I said,*" she repeated with exasperation, "there's a woman here wanting to speak to you. She claims to be your wife!"

Uh-oh. Louann must have seen something in the papers, giving his location. His ex-wife hadn't known where to find him the past year.

And by the sound of Megan's voice, he was going to have some fence-mending to do with her when this was over. "Is she tall, blond and dripping in diamonds?"

"Why, yes, she is. How did you know?"

"Just a guess," he told her, his words as sarcastic as hers. "Put her in the living room and leave her alone. I'll be there in a few minutes."

He turned to Jose. "I've got an emergency back at the house, and I don't know how long it will take."

Jose looked at his watch. "I'll circle the back pasture. If I don't find any problems, I'll push the mamas and babies toward the house and come on in."

"Good enough. Thanks, Jose."

He tucked the cell phone away and swung into the saddle. He'd like to think he could dismiss his *ex*-wife in a matter of minutes, but he had his doubts. Once she smelled money, she was hard to dislodge.

He only hoped Megan left her alone. He didn't want any sharing of confidences between the two women.

That would be a disaster.

MEGAN GAVE the woman Rick's message, at least the living room part of it.

The woman stood in the room, surveying it, a sneer on her face, and Megan forgot her own dismay when she'd first seen the room. It was out of date, and, at the time, dusty, but she and her mother had cleaned and polished. Now it looked nice.

"Bring me something to drink," the woman ordered, after sinking onto the couch with a sigh. "A martini would be nice."

"It might be nice, but all I have to offer is iced tea or grape juice." And she didn't even bother to apologize.

Another stare, this one plainly calling her an uncivilized heathen.

Megan shrugged her shoulder and started out of the room.

"Oh, all right, I'll take some iced tea."

The ungraciousness of her words made Megan consider spilling the iced tea down the front of her fire-engine red designer suit.

Instead, she counseled herself to have pity on the woman. She must be dumb as a post to have given up Rick Astin as a husband. Maybe she deserved a little pity.

A teaspoonful…maybe.

She carried a glass of iced tea back to the living room, set it down without saying anything and walked away.

As per instructions.

She finished up the icing and began to put it on the cooled cake layers, stopping only to take a tray of cookies from the oven.

She was just finishing up the cake when Torie appeared in the kitchen.

"Mommy, Drew is crying."

Megan had forgotten to turn on the baby monitor. "Oh, dear. Wait right here, sweetie, while I go get him. Then I'll fix you some milk and cookies."

"Can Flower have a cookie, too?" Torie called after her as the dog raced to the little girl's side.

"No!" Megan called back as she hurried up the stairs.

She changed Drew and brought him back to the kitchen. As she was putting him in his high chair and warning Torie not to let Flower jump up, the kitchen door swung open and their guest stared at the three of them.

"Children? Where did they come from?"

Megan glared at her and said nothing.

"Who's that?" Torie asked.

"I have no idea, sweetie. Get in your chair if you want cookies."

"How long am I supposed to wait in this Godforsaken place?'' the woman demanded at the same time.

And to top it all off, the backdoor opened and a smelly, dirty Rick stalked into the kitchen.

Torie chose that moment to complicate matters. ''Daddy! Do you want a cookie?''

''Daddy?'' the woman shrieked. ''What does she mean?''

Torie seemed unaffected by the woman's anger. ''Don't you have a daddy?''

''Oh, yeah, Torie,'' Rick drawled, ''she has a daddy. How is Mitchell, Louann? Still partying all over Texas?''

''My father is quite popular,'' she said precisely. ''Now explain this child's words.''

''I don't have to explain anything to you. Our divorce decree made that unnecessary, remember?''

''Could you two take your discussion to the living room before you upset the children?'' Megan intervened. She wanted to hear what they had to say, she admitted, but not to the point that the children were upset. They'd had enough anger and fighting in their young lives.

Rick surprised her by bending over and kissing her briefly. ''I have to clean up first,'' he said, gesturing to himself. ''We had to pull a calf. By the way, did you introduce yourself to Louann?''

''No,'' Megan said, a grim smile on her lips. ''The lady didn't seem interested in meeting the *housekeeper*.''

''Well, then, darlin', you should've explained her

mistake. You see, Louann, this isn't the house-keeper. This is my wife, Megan.''

Then he walked out of the room.

Nice exit line, Megan thought as she sighed. Then she realized the woman hadn't seemed all that surprised, which meant that she already knew who Megan was. And she also knew Rick wasn't still her husband.

''I hope you're not too shocked,'' Megan said with sugary sweetness. ''Why don't you go sit down and recover until Rick returns.''

Instead, the woman took a step forward. ''Listen, you little bimbo, he was mine first. I want him back, and I'll get him.''

Though anger coursed through her and a tiny voice inside her protested the idea, Megan remained composed. ''Well, that's between you and Rick, isn't it? If that's what he wants, there's nothing I can do to stop him.'' Then she smiled. ''But if it's not what he wants, there's not anything you can do to persuade him.''

''Darling, I can be more persuasive than you know.''

Megan chuckled and only said, ''Okay.''

''Don't laugh at me!'' the woman shrieked.

''Please go back into the living room.''

Torie's eyes were as big as saucers as she stared at the woman, and Drew was beginning to fuss, disturbed by the tension.

Megan didn't wait to see if the woman did as she'd asked. She got milk out of the refrigerator and poured some in the baby's cup and a small plastic glass for Torie. Then she gave them each two cookies.

In the meantime, Louann, as Rick had called her, continued to scream obscenities and threats. Megan picked up the pitcher on the cabinet and began to run water in it. She was not going to tolerate that kind of behavior in her house if she had to dump the entire pitcher of water on the woman's perfectly styled hair.

However, Flower took care of the situation.

Strolling unnoticed to the kitchen door where Louann stood, the dog lifted her leg and ruined the woman's expensive Italian leather shoes.

RICK, COMING DOWN the stairs, irritated by the ruckus Louann was raising, was startled by the shrill scream. He stepped up his pace, afraid Megan had done something to her. Not that he wouldn't understand, but—

When he entered the kitchen, Louann was still screaming, but no one was close to her.

"What happened?" he demanded even as he clapped a hand over his ex-wife's mouth.

No one spoke except Louann, and he couldn't understand her because of his hand over her mouth.

When he took it down, she spewed out, "That damned dog urinated all over my new shoes!"

He first looked at Megan and then Torie. "True?"

Both of them nodded, Torie with a guilty look.

He noted that Megan didn't seem at all contrite. "Then, Torie, you should apologize for your dog's behavior."

"I sorry," the child said, her bottom lip trembling.

Rick leaned over and kissed her cheek. "It's all right, sweetheart, she's just a baby."

"And Mrs. Astin owes you an apology, too, Torie," Megan said, her voice cold. "You and Drew. She used inappropriate language in front of you."

"You expect me to—" she began, outraged.

"Yes," Rick said, his voice hard. "Right now."

"Well, of course I didn't intend—I'm sorry," she ended, her voice and shoulders as stiff and cold as a northern wind blowing in.

"Now, if you'll come with me, we'll clear up whatever problem you have, and you can be on your way," Rick said, holding open the kitchen door.

"Of course, Richard, darling. We'll clear everything up," she said sweetly, but she shot Megan a malicious look over her shoulder.

You do that, Megan silently responded. If Rick Astin wanted that kind of woman, then Megan figured she was better off without him.

Then she calmed down. She knew Rick didn't want his ex-wife. He'd made that clear the first time they'd met. And no one would—unless he was swayed by money. Clearly, the woman had money. Had Rick married her because of it?

No. Rick was honest. That was the one thing she

was sure of. He didn't play games with people's emotions. He didn't take advantage of them either. He was an honest man.

With an ex-wife who claimed to still be married to him.

"More cookies," Torie called, though the words were slurred by the cookie still in her mouth.

"RICK, DARLING!" Louann cried as soon as they were in the living room, throwing herself against him, wrapping her arms around his neck. "I've missed you so!"

"Cut it out, Louann," he ordered sternly, pulling her arms down and pushing her away.

"But I have!" she insisted, scrunching her face into what he supposed she thought was a mournful pose.

To him, it made her look less attractive than ever. Unlike Megan, when she'd fought the tears that had filled her blue eyes on occasion. With good reason.

"Rick, I want you back. I want to have a baby. I'm ready to be a mother. We'll have our family, as you wanted. It will be perfect, you'll see."

"I thought I was speaking English when I introduced my wife, Louann. Didn't you hear me?"

"Surely you can't be serious. She's so...so frumpy! Darling, who would settle for day-old bread when you can have the best in the world?"

"Megan *is* the best in the world, Louann. She's got you beat all to pieces."

Anger built on her face. "How dare you! I..."

Suddenly her eyes narrowed and Rick prepared himself for the next volley.

"What did that child mean, calling you Daddy?" She crossed her arms over her chest. "Were you betraying me? Was she your mistress while you were married to me? Perfect! I'll sue you for everything you've got! No one gets away with two-timing me!"

"Like you did me? You're being ridiculous, but if you want to waste your money on a lawsuit, feel free. My attorney's name is Mac Gibbons. His office is in Cactus on the square."

"You're taunting me! But you'll be sorry. Juries don't like men who have mistresses! You'll see! I'll ruin you!"

The greed in her eyes almost made Rick laugh. So much for her professed love. He might've felt sorry for her, if he'd believed for a minute that she regretted the unhappiness of their marriage.

But all she regretted was the loss of his money.

When she slammed out the front door, he headed for the kitchen. All the trauma made him hungry, and he was sure he'd seen freshly baked cookies on the kitchen counter.

"ANY COOKIES for me?" Rick asked as he entered, almost tripping over the mop Megan was wielding in front of the door.

"I don't know," Megan drawled, stopping her work. "It depends on whether you're changing wives anytime soon."

He grinned. "Not a chance, sweetheart. You're stuck with me." He gave her another brief kiss and moved to the table. Sitting down by Drew, he pretended to bite his cookie, causing the little boy to squeal and giggle.

"Here! Bite mine!" Torie cried, laughing, snatching it back when Rick obliged.

"All right, that's enough playing. I don't want to be mopping up spilled milk, too."

"Flower would lick it up," Rick assured her. "But she'd probably consider it a reward for her bad behavior."

Megan's cheeks fired up and she looked away. "Right."

"Mommy already gave Flower some milk," Torie announced.

Megan groaned. She hadn't planned on telling Rick about her spiteful behavior.

He chuckled, drawing her gaze. "Did she? What a kind mommy."

She put the saucer of cookies in front of him. "At least I didn't feed the dog your cookies."

"I'm pleased about that. And thanks for staying calm," he added, his voice serious. "She's not easy to deal with."

Megan thought of the pitcher of water still sitting in the sink. Maybe she should think of more rewards for Flower. Another minute of Louann's screaming, and Rick wouldn't be thanking her. "Um, well—no, I guess not."

"Oops, that reminds me."

Before Megan could ask anything, Rick crossed the room to pick up the receiver on the wall phone and dialed. "Mac? This is Rick. If a blond woman, angry as hell, storms into your office and threatens to sue me, give her your card, tell her she's wasting her time and escort her out."

Megan's eyebrows soared. What was Rick talking about?

"I'm sure she'll tell you."

But Megan wanted to hear, too. She waited, hoping Mac would ask questions.

Before he could, even Megan heard Louann through the phone, her voice at its highest level. But she was too far away from the phone for Megan to be able to distinguish words. *Darn it!*

"Thanks," Rick said, raising his voice, before hanging up the phone.

"What was she going to sue for? The ranch? And why?" Megan asked, worrying that Rick might lose the one thing he loved.

"I'll tell you later," he said, seemingly unconcerned. "We may need to take Mac and Samantha out to dinner one night to make up for unleashing Louann on him, though."

"I'd enjoy that."

"Yeah, it'd be our first date," he said with a smile.

Megan stared at him in surprise. "But we're married."

"Yeah, I haven't forgotten. It came in handy

with Louann.'' He bit a cookie in half.

"Well, I'm glad I could help!'' Megan snapped.

MEGAN WANTED ANSWERS. She'd gotten over her irritation with Rick for his remark about how useful their marriage had been for him. After all, that was the purpose of their marriage. To be useful for both of them.

But he didn't get to keep secrets.

He'd said later, and she'd had no choice but to wait. She couldn't abandon the children. She had to finish up the cookies. Then there was dinner to prepare. Her mother had returned, eager to talk about her shopping trip.

But now all the chores were done, the children were in bed, her mother had retired to her bedroom with a new murder mystery she'd bought earlier. There was nothing to keep Rick from explaining.

Except that Rick, too, had retreated.

Megan headed up the stairs. Knocking on his door, she waited impatiently for him to answer.

"Megan! Is anything wrong?'' he asked as he opened his door.

Why did he sound so surprised? Who else would be knocking on his door at eight-thirty? "No, nothing's wrong, but you promised to explain about the lawsuit.''

He frowned and looked back over his shoulder.

"Do you have company?'' she asked, feeling ridiculous.

"No, of course not. I was just working on something on the computer, but I'll save it and work on it later. Just a minute.''

He didn't ask her in, so Megan stood at the door, like a formal visitor. An unhappy formal visitor.

He returned to the door. ''Want to go sit in the porch swing?''

''All right.'' She turned and hurried down the stairs.

''You got any more cookies?'' he asked as they reached the kitchen.

''You had cake after dinner.''

''Are you saying I'm getting fat?'' he asked, patting his flat, hard stomach.

Exasperated, she opened the cookie jar and held it out to him. ''No, of course not. I'm just wondering where you put it all.''

He grinned and helped himself to the cookies.

When they reached the back porch, the peaceful quiet of the night enveloped them. Rick sat and immediately put his arm on the back of the swing, curving it around her shoulders as Megan sat down.

She didn't waste any time. ''Now, tell me why Louann is suing you.''

''Thought about suing me, you mean.''

His smug look didn't supply the answers she wanted. Jabbing him in the stomach, she said, ''Tell me.''

''Ow! Okay, woman, if you're going to torture me.''

She relaxed slightly. Obviously the situation wasn't too serious, if he could tease about it.

"Actually, I owe Torie. She's the one who routed Louann."

"Torie?"

"It was Torie calling me Daddy. She thought we'd had an affair while I was married to her. She was going to sue me for being unfaithful."

"But you would never—" Megan began and then halted. She didn't know how she knew Rick would never break his wedding vows, but she did.

He leaned over and kissed her, a kiss not as brief as his earlier ones. More lingering. More sensual. More memorable. "Thanks, sweetheart, for the vote of confidence."

"So...so Mac set her straight?"

"Yeah." Then he kissed her again.

She reached up to push him away, but somehow, she lost track of her intention by the time her hand rested on his muscular chest. Instead, her fingers smoothed their way over his chest, feeling the warmth and strength of the man.

His arm curved tighter around her, and he reslanted his lips over hers, taking the kiss deeper and deeper.

When he raised his head, he whispered, "I sure am glad I'm married to you, because I don't think I could remain faithful to another woman with you in my arms."

Chapter Thirteen

Megan fought her emotions for a week.

That night on the porch, in Rick's arms, she'd almost forgotten the purpose for their marriage. The promises she'd made to herself about any man, even Rick.

She remembered the hunger she'd felt every time she got near him. The shivers that coursed through her when he'd touched her. The rightness that filled her when he'd kissed her.

There were a mass of contradictions that she didn't know what to do. She found herself staring into space, losing track of time. She even burned dinner once. Her mother was horrified to serve such a meal to Rick.

When she got to the office on Monday afternoon, she greeted Samantha cheerfully, promising herself she'd keep her mind on her work today.

"Hi," Samantha returned. "Mac wanted me to ask you if tonight would be good for the four of us to have dinner at The Last Roundup. It seems Rick promised him a dinner for dealing with the ex-wife.''

''Oh, yes, he did mention that. Tonight sounds fine for me. I'll call Mom and let her know so she won't cook a big meal.''

She also called Rick, warning him to come in earlier than usual. And then spent the rest of the afternoon trying to forget Rick's comment about tonight being their first date.

As if he wanted to change their relationship.

His kisses had indicated the same thing.

When she got home, a little after six, she only had a half hour to get ready.

''Is Rick here yet?'' she asked as she entered the kitchen.

Faith, feeding the children, said, ''He just came in. I think he's in the shower now. You want to use my bathroom downstairs?''

''Yes, thanks, Mom. And thanks for taking care of the little ones tonight.''

''You know you've given me time off, too.''

As Megan started to exit the kitchen, Faith stopped her.

''Um, Megan, do you remember the suit Rick wore when you went to Fort Worth?''

Megan frowned at the strange question. ''Of course. It was a nice blue pinstripe.''

''I was putting away his shirts in his closet today and…I didn't mean to pry, but my eye caught sight of the label.''

Megan shook her head impatiently. "What is it, Mom?"

"The label had the name Armani on it. Isn't that a really expensive suit?"

"Yes. Yes, it is," Megan agreed, remembering the disquiet she'd felt at the nice suit, the Rolex watch. The tux he owned.

Then she sighed with relief. "His wife, his ex-wife, that is, had a lot of money, I think. When she came here—"

"She came here? When? Why didn't you tell me?" Faith asked, astonished.

"It was last Tuesday, Mom. A lot happened, but it wasn't important. Anyway, she was wearing a designer suit and had lots of diamonds. She probably bought the suit for him. He also had a Rolex watch, but I'm pretty sure she bought it. He said it was a gift."

"Oh, of course. I was surprised because he accepted our offer and—if he hadn't needed money, he would've hired a housekeeper. Any man who loves to eat as much as Rick does would spend the money if he had it," Faith finished, chuckling.

"You're right. Now, I've got to hurry or I'll keep everyone waiting."

She did hurry through her shower, shampooing her hair, then rushing upstairs with it wet. She'd reviewed her wardrobe in her mind several times during the afternoon and settled on a royal-blue dress with a scooped neckline and a belt that emphasized her narrow waist.

It was ridiculous to be so nervous. She'd been living with Rick for several weeks. Tomorrow would be their two week anniversary, of their marriage.

But this was different. This was their first date.

And she could scarcely breathe from the excitement.

RICK SAT at the kitchen table, watching Faith feed Drew and chatting with Torie.

"Megan hadn't told me about your ex-wife coming. I hope there were no problems," Faith said, looking at him briefly before turning her attention back to Drew.

Rick chuckled. "Ah, Faith, you missed a real show. My ex-wife is not a nice lady."

"Sorry I missed it," she told him with a similar chuckle.

"That's why we're going out tonight. I told Mac I owed him a dinner for sending the woman to him."

"That bad, hmm?"

"The worst."

"Must make my daughter look pretty good," Faith said with a smile.

Rick paused. It would be easy to simply agree. But since that night on the porch, he knew he wasn't going to walk away. If he could help it, there would be no divorce.

"Faith, no one could look better than Megan to me."

He was relieved that she seemed pleased. She opened her mouth to say something, he didn't know what, but she stopped when the kitchen door swung open.

Megan, in a lovely blue dress that made her eyes look huge, stood there, smiling.

He rose and crossed to her, catching her chin in his fingers. "You look beautiful," he whispered, then covered her lips with his.

Torie squealed. "Me, too. Kiss me, too, Rick!"

He released Megan reluctantly. "What happened to calling me Daddy?" he asked.

"I forgot. Kiss me, too, Daddy!"

He leaned over and kissed her cheek. "You two be good for Grandma, tonight, okay?"

"We will!" Torie assured him, beaming. "We're going to watch videos."

"Aha. Smart Grandma," he said, winking at Faith. "Ready, sweetheart?" he asked Megan.

She nodded, still not speaking.

He took her hand and led her out the backdoor where he'd parked his truck.

They were halfway to the restaurant before he addressed her. "You haven't said anything. Are you unhappy about having dinner with Mac and Sam? Because she's your boss?"

"No, of course not. Samantha is wonderful."

"Well, if you don't object to them, it must be me."

Her cheeks flamed, but she hurriedly reassured

him. "Don't be silly. It's just…I'm nervous," she confessed.

Rick gave her a sharp glance. "Why?"

"It's different from being at home together."

"Ah. You mean because this is our first date?" he asked, grinning, pleased to know she remembered his words.

"Yes, but that's a ridiculous thought. We're married, for heaven's sake."

"Yeah," he agreed huskily. "But we're still newlyweds, so why don't you scoot over and use the middle seat belt."

"No. We're almost there."

But he heard the tension in her voice, saw the sideways glance she gave him, and grinned. On the way home, he'd insist.

MEGAN ENJOYED the evening. She particularly laughed at Mac's description of Louann charging into his office.

"But what did she expect to gain from it? I mean, she's the one with the money, isn't she?" she asked, looking at Rick.

He shrugged his shoulders. "She's a mean, spiteful woman."

"Then how did Mac convince her to drop it?"

Mac stepped in and answered. "My powerful arguments, my silver tongue, my persuasive voice…and the fact that I said she'd have to pay the legal costs if she failed." Then he added, "In my humble opinion, some rich people are the stingiest I've ever met.''

''That's terrible,'' Megan protested. ''Money isn't important in itself. It's what it can do. I mean, look at Dr. Greenfield's wife. She sponsors those parenting classes for all the young people in the county. That can make a real difference to a child's future.''

Rick didn't know about the classes and asked several questions. They all agreed Florence's classes were wonderful. Samantha had gone to them several evenings to offer her expertise.

''If you had money, what else would you do?'' Rick asked Megan.

She shrugged her shoulders, then said, ''I'd offer scholarships to students who reached a certain grade point in their high-school career. Maybe combine that requirement with public service. Or provide the local schools with computer equipment so the students have a chance in the real world at getting jobs.''

Samantha agreed enthusiastically. ''Or how about free child care to young single mothers? They can't make enough to afford good child care. It's too expensive.''

''Yes, and there's—''

The two women were off and running, with many ideas for improving the community.

Mac leaned across to Rick. ''I think Megan should run for mayor. She'd do a heck of a job running the town.''

Megan overheard him. ''No, I wouldn't. Right now I have to concentrate on raising Torie and Drew. But maybe after they're grown?'' she suggested with a grin.

''But don't you and Rick plan to have children?'' Samantha asked, then turned bright red. ''Oh! I'm sorry. I mean—you seem so natural together. I didn't intend to—oh, I'm making a mess out of everything, aren't I?'' She hid her face on her husband's shoulder.

''It's okay, honey,'' Mac assured her, grinning. ''If they sue, I know a really good lawyer.''

She raised her head and slapped his arm, grinning. ''Thanks a lot. I really am sorry.''

Megan graciously accepted the apology. Rick, on the other hand, put his arm around Megan and drawled, ''Don't give up on us, Samantha. We may surprise you yet.''

Megan's cheeks burned and she avoided looking at anyone. How could Rick make such a remark? They hadn't…it was their first date!

When she realized her ridiculous thought, she gave a prayer of gratitude that she hadn't said the words aloud. They'd think she was crazy.

''Good for you,'' Mac said with a laugh.

Suddenly, Jessica and Cal appeared at their table.

''Well, well, well,'' Cal said. ''Out partying and you didn't invite us?''

Rick and Mac, in a convoluted dialogue, explained the reason behind the dinner and then invited Cal and Jessica to join them. Soon it was a party of six, instead of four.

Megan found herself relaxing. She forgot the problems with her niece and nephew. She forgot the confusion she felt about Rick. She felt carefree for the first time in a year, since before her sister's death.

Finally, Rick called a halt to the evening. "Sorry to have to break this up, but I don't have office hours like you guys. I have to get up early in the morning."

"Ha! We've heard that before from Spence and Tuck," Cal assured him, naming the friends with ranches near Rick's. "You know, we need to have a barbecue soon. We haven't had one since Alex and Tuck's wedding."

"That sounds great," Samantha agreed. "But have it soon before I get too big to be seen in public."

Everyone protested except Mac who leaned over to whisper something in his wife's ear. She turned a bright red and slapped his arm again.

"Amazing, isn't it?" Cal teased. "They're still acting like newlyweds."

"Like you two are any different," Mac protested.

Megan felt envy well up in her. One of the nicest things about moving to Cactus was making friends with these couples. And seeing the bliss of their marriages. She hadn't really believed it was possible to have such happiness anymore.

Not after her sister's disaster of a marriage.

Cal looked at her and Rick. "Of course, you two have an excuse."

"What's that?" Rick asked.

"You *are* newlyweds," Cal pointed out with a laugh.

Rick assured them he hadn't forgotten. Then he stood and pulled Megan to her feet, wrapping his arm around her.

She didn't protest. After all, she knew he was posturing for his friends, for the reputation of their marriage. Besides, his arm felt too good around her.

When they left the restaurant, Jessica and Cal stayed behind so she could check on something in the kitchen. As owner, she kept close tabs on everything.

Mac and Samantha continued out of the restaurant with Rick and Megan.

"Uh, guys, I hate to end the evening on a bad note, but I do have something I need to discuss with you," Mac said in a low voice as they went down the steps.

Megan spun around, her gaze anxious. Rick's arm steadied her.

"What is it, Mac?" he asked, his voice serious.

"The P.I. I hired called late this afternoon. He hasn't been able to find much on Moody. It's common knowledge that his father has paid off a lot of people, but he can't find anyone to talk."

"But maybe he still can?" Megan asked, thinking the news wasn't as dismal as she'd thought it might be.

"Maybe. But that's not the bad news."

They stood silently, waiting, braced for what Mac would say next.

"He heard there's a possibility Moody may be released early."

"How?" Rick demanded.

"It seems a certain judge pulled some strings."

Megan's hand covered her mouth, but not before everyone heard her moan. "How—how early?"

"In a week or two."

"But he had another three months to serve!" she protested.

"I know. I'm sorry, Megan."

She couldn't say anything else. Biting her bottom lip to keep from crying, she nodded and turned to Rick's truck. She had to get away.

Rick shook Mac's hand, nodded to Samantha, and hurried after her. She slid into the front seat. Before she could close the door, he nudged her. "Sit in the middle. We need to talk."

As an excuse, it was lame, but she felt so cold, so shaken, that closeness to Rick sounded just about perfect right now. She did as he ordered.

He slid in the truck and wrapped his right arm around her as he started the truck and backed out of the parking lot. Megan tried to remain calm, but she began shaking as reaction set in.

"Shh, baby, it's all right," he whispered before his lips touched her forehead.

"I'm frightened, Rick. He's...he'll make trouble."

"We'll protect the kids, sweetheart. We're going to make this come out right, I promise."

Megan loved his words. She appreciated his support. But she wasn't sure she believed him. She and her mother had been fighting Drake Moody ever since they realized how he was treating Andrea. It had been an uphill battle.

Now it seemed as if they were facing a cliff.

No way out.

Tears filled her eyes, but she struggled not to let them escape. Torie's sweet little face swam in her mind. Drew's innocence filled her heart. She had to protect the children.

And Rick was willing to help.

She lay her head on his shoulder. "Thank you," she whispered. "Thank you for always being there for me. Thank you for being the opposite of Drake Moody."

"My pleasure," he said softly and continued to drive.

HOLDING MEGAN TIGHTLY against him was having the usual effect on his body. Rick called himself an animal to even think of sex at a time like this.

He damn well was going to make sure that judge lost the election come November. He'd call his business manager tomorrow and set things in motion. The man's opponent would have everything legally possible to win.

In the meantime, their wonderful evening had ended in disaster. Not that it was Mac's fault. At least they'd had a good time. But the pleasure he'd felt, sharing dinner with friends, showing off his beautiful lady, making plans in his head for other evenings to lure her into his arms, had all disappeared.

He stopped beside the back porch and got out, turning to pull Megan after him. She slid into his arms and he swung her up against his chest to carry her inside.

"Rick, I'm frightened."

"I know you are. So am I. But that's the smart thing to be. It keeps you alert, on your toes. It keeps you battle-ready. If you're too complacent, you're sure to lose."

"You sound like you've fought a lot of battles."

"Yeah, I have. And we're going to fight this one, too. Okay?"

He felt her head nod against his neck, but she said nothing. After he'd gotten them in the house, he set her down to lock the backdoor. Then he took her hand and led her up the stairs.

"Why don't you sleep in tomorrow morning," he suggested. "I can make my own breakfast."

"No. You've given me so much, I...I can never repay you. I made the best bargain in the world when I asked you to marry me."

"No, sweetheart, I made the best bargain. And I never intend to let you go. There will be no annulment. When you're ready, this marriage is going to be real…in every way. But we'll wait until everything's calmed down and you've had time to think.''

He was proud of himself. He wanted her so badly he could barely walk straight, but now was not the time to sway her. He didn't want her thinking he would take advantage of her.

She'd said nothing, so he leaned down and kissed her forehead and nudged her toward her bedroom door. With a sigh.

''Are you sure?'' she asked, her head still down.

''Sure? About our marriage?'' He drew a deep breath. ''Oh, yeah, I'm sure.''

''I'll always have Torie and Drew. They're my children now.''

''And mine. Torie calls me Daddy, remember?''

''But, Rick, it's different when it's pretend.''

He couldn't stop. He pulled her against him and kissed her lips. ''Sweetheart, it hasn't been pretend for me for a long time.''

''It hasn't?''

He lifted her chin and looked into her eyes. ''Megan, we'd better cut this short if you intend to be a virgin in the morning. I don't want to take advantage of your stress. I want you to come to me because it's what you want.''

Her arms slid around his neck and she leaned her body flush against his. ''It's what I want, Rick.''

''You're sure?''

''Do I have to beg? I want to be with you. I want to wake beside you in the morning. I've finally found a man I can respect, an honest man, a decent man. I'm sure.''

And he'd found an honest and decent woman, who also happened to be beautiful and sexy. As his lips descended to hers, his mind traveled over her words and tripped over the honest part.

But he'd explain. She'd understand.

Tomorrow, he'd tell her the truth.

Because he couldn't think of anything but making love to Megan tonight.

Chapter Fourteen

Rick carried Megan into his bedroom and carefully placed her on the king-size bed. He'd dreamed of sharing his bed with her for the past two weeks.

From the first, he'd been attracted to her. He supposed that was why he'd agreed to her offer so quickly, in spite of his fears of marriage. She was hard to resist.

Before he could pull away, Megan tugged him down, her lips seeking his. He didn't hesitate to follow her lead because kissing her was something he craved. As their lips mated, their kiss growing deeper and deeper, his hands ran over her body, tracing her curves, stroking her.

His hands slid beneath her skirt, but her warm flesh was shielded by the pantyhose she wore. Frustrated, hungering to touch her, he lifted his lips. "Megan, I want to touch you."

She sat up and reached for her zipper. Rick eagerly assisted her. Pulling her dress over her head, she flung it away. But instead of working on disrobing herself anymore, she reached for the buttons on Rick's shirt. And her lips returned to his.

The undressing took awhile because it was hard to remove their clothing unless they separated. And neither could stop the touching, the kissing, long enough to complete the job. Yet, both continued to work on it.

"Rick, I'm burning up," Megan confessed, stroking his chest, now that she'd removed his shirt. When her hand strayed to the belt buckle, he drew in a deep breath.

"Me, too," he whispered and took her lips again.

Megan's hand slipped below his belt, feeling the hard ridge beneath his zipper. With a moan, she returned to the belt buckle, working at unfastening it.

Suddenly it seemed urgent for him to help her. Once his jeans were discarded, he stripped her of her panties, the last obstacle to their mating. Then he poised himself over her.

Mindful of her inexperience, he eased his way between her legs, still stroking and kissing her with all his being, wanting her to suffer as little as possible. When he finally pushed into her, he held her tightly, whispering sweet words into her ears before his lips returned to hers.

MEGAN HAD expected the pain, but it was soon lost in Rick's care of her, in his touch, his caress, his kiss. Her desire returned tenfold as he began to move in her. She clung tightly, urging him on, unable to bear the thought of halting the most beautiful experience of her life.

When she thought she could stand the shimmering, electrical sensations no longer, she felt a starburst of release that shone in her mind like a fireworks display. Then felt a rapid descent into utter exhaustion.

Rick, too, stilled, his body lying damp and heavy on hers. But rather than crush her, he seemed as one with her, a feeling of completion she'd never felt before.

"Megan? Are you all right? Did I hurt you?"

She couldn't speak, but she shook her head no.

"You're not all right?" he asked anxiously, raising up on one arm.

"I'm...wonderful," she whispered, still discovering it difficult to find words.

Rick rolled off her, making her want to protest, until he pulled her to him as he lay beside her. Wrapped in his arms, she felt she'd come home, to the one place in the world that was hers.

"Rick, I..." What could she say? Words couldn't explain the emotions coursing through her, faster than light. She wanted to tell him so much— and she wanted to say nothing.

His lips covered hers, a gentle kiss that spoke of love, not lust. And she decided he understood. Her eyelids fluttered down and she let exhaustion claim her.

RICK HELD her against him long after she slept. He pulled the covers over the two of them, savoring their togetherness.

Just as he'd known, soon after his first marriage, that he'd made a mistake, this time he knew, too. That he'd made a glorious decision when he'd married Megan Ford. Megan Astin.

He liked saying her name, his name. And he intended to hold her to him for the rest of her life. She was his soul mate, his partner, the perfect woman for him. He loved her more than life itself.

Though he drifted to sleep, he awoke several hours later and gently awakened Megan by his hands roaming her body, touching at will what had once been forbidden territory. He delighted in her response, her willingness to touch him, to join him in their loving.

Though he wasn't sure she ever came fully awake.

When the alarm rang before dawn, he tried to slip from the bed without awakening her. As he withdrew his warmth, she moaned and reached for him, her eyes still closed. He rewarded her with a soft kiss.

Then he left the bed, knowing he'd carry the experiences of the night with him all day, until he could touch her again.

MEGAN DIDN'T get to sleep in all that much later, since Drew awakened her at his normal time, a little before seven.

She was disappointed to find Rick gone, but not

surprised. Her husband was a hard worker. She savored the word *husband* with pride.

"Drew, Daddy is such a good man," she told the little boy as she put him in the high chair. It was the first time she'd actually acknowledged aloud what she'd recognized for a few days. Rick was a terrific father.

He'd coaxed Torie from her fear of men. Now she ran to Rick when he came into sight. He'd begun to pay more attention to Drew, too, as if finally realizing he too was a person, even though he didn't speak.

Sometimes Megan worried that Drew wasn't making much effort to speak, but her mother assured her that often happened with the second child. Torie spoke for both of them.

She fixed Drew's breakfast and celebrated the day by letting him try to feed himself. Though it was a messy experience, she and Drew were both pleased by the process.

In fact, after she put him in the playpen they'd set up in the kitchen, she cleaned the room, singing as she moved.

Faith and Torie came in together an hour later.

"My, someone's in a good mood," Faith commented, a smile on her face. "Your evening must've been pleasurable."

Megan's immediate thoughts brought a bright blush to her cheeks. Then she remembered the rest of the evening. "Yes, we…we had a nice evening. But Mac had some bad news for me." She lowered her voice even more. "Drake may be out of prison soon."

Faith had begun to prepare breakfast for herself and Torie. Now she stopped, her eyes wide. "When?"

"Maybe in a week or two," Megan whispered.

"I'm hungry!" Torie announced from the table, already in place, watching her aunt and grand-mother.

"Coming right up, sweetie," Megan assured her. Then she squeezed her mother's shoulder in silent support of her fears.

They both worked through their concerns, quietly talking when the children were occupied, cleaning the house as they did. Megan had repeated Rick's assurances, hoping they comforted her mother as much as they did her.

She had just started preparing lunch when the phone rang.

"Is Mr. Astin there?"

"He's outside working. May I take a message?"

"Who's speaking, please?"

With a thrill that she attempted to hide, she said, "This is his wife, Megan."

"Oh, yes. This is his business manager, Gerald Roberts. I need to talk to him about the opportunities in Fort Worth. I think the mayor has something he'll be interested in. And also there are some bills from a Mac Gibbons, Attorney-at- Law, I need his approval on. When will he be in?"

"He should be in for lunch."

"Great. And, uh, I'm afraid a reporter may have gotten his phone number from me by accident." The man really sounded nervous now, and Megan wondered if this fact had been the real reason for the call.

"A reporter?"

"Yes, I'm sure Rick has told you to make no comment if someone calls or comes out."

"Is this about the custody battle?" she asked sharply. The mayor of Fort Worth had been at the custody hearing, she remembered. And that was the only reason for a reporter to want to contact Rick. But how would they know about his business manager. And why did he have one? And why hadn't he mentioned that fact to her?

"No. The reporters have all been trying to find him since he disappeared last year. The custody battle gave them a clue. I told him he shouldn't have appeared in public."

"He disappeared?" Her mind was spinning with all the information she was receiving. Information she wasn't sure she wanted. It was bursting the bubbles of her happy future.

Suddenly, the man sounded unsure of himself. "Uh, surely he's told you—I mean, you're aware of his past, aren't you, Mrs. Astin? About CAP Computers?"

"No, Mr. Roberts, I'm not, but you can tell me." Her voice had grown hard. After all, the biggest bubble of all, her husband's honesty, had just burst all over her.

"Uh, no, I don't think—tell your husband to call me, please." And he hung up.

Megan slowly replaced the receiver and leaned against the wall, her eyes closed.

"Megan? Is something wrong?" Faith asked, coming to her side.

"I don't know. I need to go upstairs for a minute. Can you watch the kids?"

"Sure. Shall I go ahead with preparing lunch?"

"Please, Mom, thanks. I'll be down in a few minutes."

Once she reached the top of the stairs, she entered Rick's room, not hers. The room she'd shared with him last night and felt such complete happiness.

But it wasn't the bed that drew her this morning. It was the computer. A CAP computer.

She wasn't a computer expert, but she knew how to operate one. And how to search the Internet for information.

In a matter of minutes, she had more information than she ever wanted on that company…and the man who'd created it, Richard Astin.

And sold it for an incredible amount of money before disappearing.

But she knew more than appeared on the screen. Because she knew where billionaire Richard Astin was, and what he was doing with his life. She didn't know why, but she knew where.

And she also knew he wasn't what he'd appeared to be when she'd proposed to him, offering him five thousand dollars to marry her. He must've laughed his head off.

Why had he agreed? He could afford a hundred housekeepers and never notice the money spent. Instead he'd accepted her offer and taken on her and her family.

And last night he'd made love to her.

Or had sex with her.

He hadn't said he loved her. Just that he didn't want the marriage to end. After all, he liked her cooking. And she appeared to be an apt pupil in bed.

As he'd said, quite a bargain.

What was it Mac had said about wealthy people? Many of them were stingier than the average person. Rick must've figured he should get more for the bargain he'd made. Cooking wasn't enough.

She turned off the computer, tears streaming down her cheeks. She hurried to the bathroom to wash her face and compose herself before she faced her mother.

As she entered the kitchen, the phone rang again. She waved to her mother as she picked up the receiver. "Hello?"

"Is this Rick Astin's residence?"

"I think you have the wrong number," she said, trying to sound disinterested.

"Wait! Who's speaking?"

She hung up the receiver.

"Who was that?" Faith asked.

"Wrong number. And if the phone rings again, I'll—"

It did. She lifted the receiver. "Hello?"

"Don't hang up. I'm sure—"

She hung up. "Same person."

"I've got lunch almost ready. You want to wash Torie's face and hands? Is Rick coming in for lunch today?"

Megan closed her eyes. Facing Rick was going to be difficult. As she contemplated that disaster, the phone rang again.

"I told you—" she began.

"Megan? It's Cal. Is everything all right?"

"Yes, yes, sorry. I thought you were a wrong number."

"Oh," he said, chuckling. "Those can be annoying."

"Yes."

"Look, I'm calling because a social worker stopped by to get directions to your house. Seems the court in Fort Worth has sent her out to do a home observation. I'm going to bring her out and, uh, Rick suggested I be an extra witness, you know?"

"He knew she was coming?"

"Yeah, didn't the judge say someone would?"

"Oh." She'd meant today, but obviously Rick had made the suggestion when they'd gotten back to Cactus, before she arrived. "I appreciate it, Cal. Are you coming now? Shall we set two extra places for lunch?"

"Hey, that'd be great. We're on our way."

Megan hung up the phone. "Mom, there'll be two more for lunch. Is there enough food?"

"Yes, of course. I made extra, thinking we'd have leftover meatloaf later in the week. Who's coming?"

"The social worker and Cal. I'll set the table."

After doing so, she took both children upstairs to clean up for lunch, all the while trying to make sense of a suddenly upside-down world.

She couldn't say anything to Rick about his lies while the social worker was present. She couldn't demand an explanation for his actions. She couldn't scream and rage at him as she wanted to do.

Should she give him the message from Gerald Roberts?

She supposed she should, the man had said it was important. Apparently more important than her and their life together. After all, the man hadn't been surprised with her identity, so he must know about her.

But she'd had no idea he even existed.

The happiness with which she'd awakened this morning seemed so long ago and so foreign to the confusion and heartache she now felt, Megan could scarcely remember it. But she had to pretend a marital bliss that wasn't possible, a happy home that didn't exist, a united front of parental responsibility.

So she could keep the children.

While she wiped Drew's face and hands and supervised Torie's enthusiastic splashing, she shored up her defenses and her courage. It was going to be a long lunch.

RICK DIDN'T always come in for lunch, but he wouldn't have missed today's for anything. He hungered for more than food. He wanted to touch Megan again, to hold her against him. To kiss her.

He wanted to be sure she was feeling okay. The first time she experienced sex could be traumatic for a woman. And he wanted to tell her he loved her.

Saying those words wouldn't be easy. But he regretted not saying them during the night. He wanted her to know that she had his love, his devotion. And he wanted to hear her say the same thing to him.

He discovered the kitchen empty except for Faith when he came in. "Hi, where's everyone?"

Faith had a slight frown on her face. "Megan and the children are upstairs, cleaning up for lunch. And you'd better, too. The social worker and Cal are coming to eat with us."

"Okay. Thanks, Faith."

Cleaning up wasn't what chased him up the stairs double-time. He rushed because he wanted to see Megan. But as he reached the top of the stairs, she and the children were coming down.

"Hi, sweetheart," he said enthusiastically, grabbing her for a quick kiss.

She pulled away and, grabbing Torie's hand, brushed past him.

"Megan?"

"Wait!" Torie squealed. "I want Daddy to kiss me, too."

"Later," Megan said, never stopping.

"Megan, what's wrong?"

"The social worker's on her way."

And that was the only explanation he got. Panic streamed through his veins. He'd been right to worry. Megan was unhappy.

He dashed into the bathroom for a quick washup. Maybe it was the sudden appearance of the social worker that had frightened her. He'd done what he could to protect her by asking Cal to come as a witness.

That must be what it was. Megan was thinking about the social worker and had set aside her private life. He felt a little reassured at his deduction. After all, he'd seen Megan shut him out before when she'd been worried about the children.

After the social worker departed, they'd talk. He'd explain that he was on her side, always. That they should share their concerns. She'd agree.

That's what marriage was all about, sharing the good times and the bad.

Even though he hurried, Cal and the social worker were coming in the backdoor when he got to the kitchen. There would be no talking to Megan now.

MEGAN DREW A deep breath and calmly greeted Cal. Then she extended a hand to the woman beside him.

"Thank you for coming. I hope it wasn't too hard a trip."

The woman smiled, seeming friendly. "Not at all. I'm delighted because it gives me an excuse to visit family in Lubbock."

Megan introduced the children and her mother, then Rick. She'd known the moment he entered the kitchen, but she hadn't acknowledged his presence until now.

"I believe lunch is ready. Why don't we go ahead and eat and then you can ask whatever questions are necessary and look around the house."

They all sat down, Torie insisting on her now customary place beside Rick.

"Daddy, you didn't kiss me like you did Mommy," she immediately complained.

Rick leaned over and kissed her cheek. "Sorry, angel, Mommy was in a hurry."

Megan noted the social worker's observation and drew a deep breath. Torie was being a good witness without any prompting.

The next hour was nerve-wracking. After the meal, the woman asked a lot of questions. Rick never suggested he go back out to work, taking it for granted he should remain for the questioning.

Megan had hoped he'd excuse himself. Instead, he sat at the cleared table. He even reached out and clasped hands with her after Torie had gone to go play. She'd tried to hide her reaction, a sudden clenching of her nerves.

The woman hadn't noticed, but she knew Rick had.

Finally, the woman stood. "Well, that's all the questions. All I need now is to see the rest of your home. Then I'll be on my way. Mr. Astin, if you want to get back to work, that will be fine."

Rick hesitated, but Megan prayed he'd leave. She couldn't maintain her calm exterior much longer.

"Okay, thanks." He leaned over and kissed Megan before rising and striding to the door.

Suddenly, she couldn't stand his hypocrisy any longer. Rising, she said, "Excuse me just a moment. I forgot to give my husband a telephone message.

"Rick?" she called as she reached the back porch.

He spun around, surprise on his face. Then he hurried to her, his arms outstretched.

She stepped back and he frowned, her message clear. "You had a phone call. Gerald Roberts, your business manager, asked that you call him right away."

Her words must've given him a clue to the frost in her gaze. He reached for her again. "Megan..."

She took another step back, avoiding him. "He said it was important."

Then she turned and went into the house.

Chapter Fifteen

Rick tried to think.

How much had Gerald revealed? Rick wanted to head back into the house, grab Megan and demand she talk to him. But the social worker was still there. He couldn't do anything to risk the children.

He hurried to the barn and pulled the cellular phone out of his saddlebag. He'd approach the problem from another angle, Gerald.

A few minutes' conversation with the man told Rick Megan knew enough to be upset. He wanted to fire Gerald. But he didn't. The man had served him well for a number of years. He couldn't blame his lack of honesty on Gerald.

"I hope I didn't cause any problems. I didn't mean for your number to get out."

"Don't worry about it," Rick said wearily. "I'll have to change the number, but I'll let you know the new one. Only keep it locked up, okay?"

"I promise, Rick."

Rick quickly dialed the local phone company, requesting a change of number, unlisted.

He debated what to do next. Though he considered going back out to work, he decided to do some chores in the barn, waiting until Megan finished with the social worker.

He settled down in the tack room, mending some of the equipment that had suffered wear and tear. As a boy, he'd done a lot of that work, under his father's tutelage. His father had assumed Rick would follow in his footsteps, running the small family farm.

Rick had discovered a talent for computers, however, an intuitive understanding and an excitement he couldn't ignore. He figured his dad would be amused if he could see him now.

As he worked on the pliant leather, the familiar scent bringing comfort, his mind turned to his present situation. He knew he owed Megan an apology and an explanation. But what they'd shared, not only last night but during the past two weeks, had to count for something.

She would give him a chance to explain.

A few minutes later, he picked up the cell phone and called the house.

"Hi, Faith, it's Rick. Is Megan there?"

"No, Rick, she had to go to work, remember?" Faith sounded impatient.

"I forgot. Is everything all right?"

"No. I'm going crazy answering the phone. Megan told me to say no comment to any questions, but for some reason, a lot of strangers are calling for you. What's going on?"

"Sorry, Faith, I'll be right there."

"Where are you?"

"In the barn. Hang on. I'll take over the phone as soon as I can."

It was time to face his past and hope he could link it to the future. With Megan.

THE CONCENTRATION required for her job helped Megan get through the rest of the day. When all the patients were gone and her duties completed, she took a moment to gather herself together.

"Are you all right?" Samantha asked. The doctor had come into the last examining room without Megan hearing her.

"Of course," Megan said at once, offering a weak smile. "How are you feeling? Is the pregnancy still making you tired?"

"So-so. Megan, are you sure everything's all right? Today you seemed tense."

It was tempting, so tempting, to tell Samantha her problems. But she couldn't. Whatever his reasons, this was Rick's home. She might leave after she gained custody of the children, probably would leave, because she couldn't bear being around Rick without... "No, nothing's wrong. The social worker came today, but I think everything went well."

"What did she say?" Samantha asked eagerly.

"When she left, she said she thought our home was perfect, and the children were well-adjusted. She couldn't see any problems."

"That's wonderful. Do you mind if I tell Mac?"

"Of course not, though probably Cal turned over the tape."

"What tape?"

"After she left, Cal pulled out a mini tape recorder. He said he and Rick had decided to record her visit in case there was any, uh, undue influence when she wrote the report."

"You mean like with the judge?" Samantha asked thoughtfully.

"Yes," Megan said with a sigh. Another reason to be grateful to Rick. Not what she needed.

"Mac said he thought the only reason the hearing went so well was Rick making sure the reporters and the mayor were there," Samantha added, matching her sigh. "It's discouraging to see so many corrupt people, isn't it?"

Megan bowed her head. More gratitude. "I certainly chose the right man to marry, didn't I?"

Instead of answering, Samantha studied her. Then she asked, "Have things changed? I mean, are you getting to know each other?"

Hysterical laughter rose in Megan. Getting to know each other? Oh, yeah. "Uh, yes, but—but we're going to hold to the agreement. When I get custody of the children, we'll get a divorce."

She should've known better than to say anything. She was too distracted to watch herself. After all, she was talking to a medical doctor and the wife of a lawyer. Samantha picked up on her words at once.

"A divorce? Not an annulment?"

Damn, damn, damn. She could feel her face flooding with color. Unable to face Samantha, she looked away.

"Oh, Megan, I'm sorry, I didn't mean to pry. It's none of my business…but I can certainly understand how…Mac was impossible to resist, even though I had a lot of reasons to. If you need me to prescribe birth control pills, just let me know." She reached over and hugged Megan, then left the room.

Birth control pills.

Had Rick used a condom?

Admittedly, she was inexperienced, but she hadn't noticed if he'd done so.

Had she been so stupid as to risk a pregnancy with a man who had promised to divorce her? Or annul her or whatever it was called?

Apparently she had.

She rubbed her forehead, hoping to ease the intensifying headache that was throbbing between her eyes.

Suddenly, she decided she couldn't go home. Not now. She needed some time to think. To prepare herself to face Rick.

She grabbed the phone and dialed their number.

"Hello?" Rick answered.

She struggled to speak. "I want to speak to Mom."

"Megan? When are you coming home? I've been waiting for—"

"I need to speak to Mom."

She shuddered with relief when her mother spoke into the phone.

"Hello, dear. Are you all right?"

"I'm fine, but I'm going to assist with Florence's class tonight, Mom, if that's all right. Can you manage the children by yourself?"

"Of course, dear, but...but Rick told me...are you sure you're all right?"

"I'm fine. I'll be home around ten."

AFTER DINNER and the children's bedtime, Rick sat down with Faith and gave her the complete explanation of his past, and why he'd accepted their proposal. It sounded silly now, that he'd been operating his ranch on a limited budget to see if he could make a success of it. To challenge himself. Knowing all the time he had enough money to operate a ranch ten times its size with all the help he wanted.

But his life had been a mess. He'd buried himself in his work because his marriage had been a disaster. His wife had divorced him because she didn't think he had enough money for her, or time. Then he'd sold his company, leaving himself with nothing to do. His parents were dead. He'd been alone.

He'd needed a new life.

Hard work and a friendly community had given him peace, if not happiness. It had taken Megan and her family to bring him that.

Faith had been understanding and sympathetic, he thought, because he didn't tell her what had happened last night.

"I'm sure Megan will eventually forgive you, Rick, but—well, Drake was such a liar. He hid a lot of things from Andrea and us. It won't be easy for Megan."

"No, I know. But my intentions were good, Faith. And I love your daughter. I don't intend to let her walk away from me, from what we have."

"It has to be Megan's decision, Rick," Faith said, leaning forward. "You see, Drake didn't give Andrea any choice, either. Nothing would scare Megan away faster than trying to force her."

"I didn't mean—thanks, Faith, for the good advice. I assume you don't have any objections if it's Megan's choice?"

"Of course not. You've been wonderful. The children and I consider you family. If Megan is happy…" Her voice trailed off and she sighed. "I love living here."

Rick smiled, hoping he could keep all of them living there. If he couldn't, he vowed he'd be the one to leave. He couldn't live there without Megan now.

"I'll do my best," he assured his mother-in-law.

Faith went up to bed, leaving Rick to await Megan's return.

As the clock neared ten, he grew more and more nervous. Finally, he moved to the porch, sitting in the porch swing in darkness, awaiting her return.

When headlights appeared on the road, he held his breath. The car turned into their drive and he watched as Megan parked the car and got out. She was only a shadow in the dark, but her outline was that of a defeated woman. Her shoulders slumped, and she walked slowly, as if she had no strength left.

And she never saw him.

He waited until she reached the back door to speak.

"Megan."

She whipped around, startled. "Rick! I didn't see you."

"Join me in the swing?"

"No. I'm tired. I'm going to bed." As she finished speaking, she turned to enter the house.

"What bed are you going to sleep in?" he asked quietly, though he already knew the answer.

After a tense silence, she said softly, "Mine. I'm going to sleep in mine."

"Megan, can't we talk? I'd like to explain why—"

"We'll talk," she assured him, her voice tight. "But not tonight. I can't, tonight."

He wanted to hold her, to comfort her, as he'd done at other times. He wanted to love her. But the desperation in her voice told him she would accept nothing from him right now.

"Okay," he agreed and watched relief in her sagging body. "When?"

"I can't...I can't think, right now. Give me a couple of days...please."

He couldn't resist her plea. He loved her. With a quiet acceptance, he nodded.

She went into the house, shutting the door behind her.

He only hoped she hadn't locked it.

THE TELEPHONE company called the next morning with their new number. Abruptly, the phone calls stopped. Rick gave the new number to Faith, and through her to Megan, and cautioned them about whom they gave it to.

Megan had gone in to work. Rick had waited for her to come down that morning. It had been a wasted effort. She'd looked pale, drawn. She hadn't eaten anything, though he'd offered to fix breakfast.

She also had scarcely spoken to him.

Faith, also up, had waited until Megan left. "Your talk didn't go well?"

"We didn't talk. She asked for a couple of days to...to think." He shrugged his shoulders. "I agreed."

"That was kind of you. And wise. I'm sure she'll listen to you soon."

Rick shrugged his shoulders again. What choice did he have?

"What are you going to do today? Aren't you going to work?"

"I'm going to hire some more help, so I don't have to put in so many hours. And I've got some projects to work on. My business manager has located an opportunity in Fort Worth that I want to look into."

"You're moving to Fort Worth?" Faith asked, startled.

"No. I'm not moving anywhere unless...I can run it from here, visiting Fort Worth only two or three times a year. But it would provide some jobs, be a challenge to me."

"Cactus could use a few more jobs, too. Mabel and I were talking the other day about our young people leaving to find jobs in Lubbock."

Rick frowned. "You're right, Faith. I'll keep that in mind." The project in Fort Worth involved hardware for the future. But he had an idea for a software program, too. Maybe he could start it up here, in Cactus.

He went up to his bedroom, where his computer was. If they all stayed...when they all settled in, he might add onto the house, build an office where he could work without leaving home.

Before he started work, he called Mac to give him his new number.

"I've been trying to reach you," Mac said at once, "and the number rang without any answer."

"Sorry, I had to change the number. Some reporters got the old one and wouldn't stop calling."

"Things are happening fast. I had word that Moody got out of prison last night. He could be on his way here."

"What? That fast? Damn! Have you told Megan?"

"No, I wanted to talk to you first. Cal and I discussed the situation. We think it would be best if

Faith and the children were hidden away somewhere until we're sure what Moody is going to do.''

"That's a good idea. I can fly them—''

"Cal's mother offered to have them visit her.''

"Here in Cactus? Do you think that's wise?''
Rick had thought he could send them on vacation.
He didn't believe Moody really wanted the children
or cared about them enough to travel very far.

"I'm not sure Megan would stand for them to go
far away,'' Mac said. "You can ask her but—''

"She'd agree if it meant their safety. I could send
her with them.''

"I thought about that, but I think she'll have to
confront Moody at some point. Better to get it over
with.''

"I won't have her in danger,'' Rick protested.

"She won't be. Cal will provide protection. The
man won't be able to find your place without asking
directions. So we'll have advance warning.''

Rick sighed. He didn't like what was happening,
but his choices were limited. "Okay, what do I
need to do?''

"Talk to Faith and Megan. Have Faith pack
some things and get her and the kids over to Mabel's right away. Megan will have to stay away
from them for a few days, to make sure she isn't
followed.

"And give Cal your new number so he can let
you know what he hears.''

"Right.''

After talking to Cal, Rick hurried back down the

stairs. "Faith," he called. She answered him from the kitchen.

He explained Mac's plan. When she hurried out of the kitchen to pack some necessities, he picked up the phone and dialed the clinic's number.

Without trying to talk to Meg, he asked for Samantha. "I'm sorry to bother you," he said when she came on the line, "but I don't think Megan will talk to me." Then he explained what was happening.

A minute later, Megan got on the phone. "Is Mom okay with the plan?" Her voice was strained, filled with worry.

"Yeah. You won't be able to see them for a few days, Megan. Okay?"

"Yes, I understand. I need to talk to her."

"I'll get her."

He waited while Faith talked to her daughter. The only part Faith had had a problem with was Megan staying behind, in case Drake appeared. Rick had promised her he would protect Megan.

He would promise the same to Megan, if she'd speak to him.

Faith hung up the phone. "Torie's choosing a few toys to take with her. Will you see if she's ready while I get Drew?"

"Sure."

In Torie's room, he discovered all her toys piled on her bed. "What's this?" he asked.

She spun around and raced to him, throwing her

arms around his legs. "Don't you love me anymore?"

He reached down and lifted the little girl into his arms. "Of course I love you. Why would you ask that?"

"Because Grandma said we have to go away," she told him, her eyes sad.

"Just for a few days, sweetheart. To keep you safe."

"But who will keep you safe? And Mommy?"

He'd already said too much. Faith hadn't wanted to alarm Torie by mentioning her father.

"I'll keep me and Mommy safe, I promise."

"And Flower?"

"And Flower. And I'll try to teach Flower not to have accidents while you're gone."

"I don't want to go. I want to stay here with you and Mommy and Flower," she pleaded, her little hands on each side of his face.

He kissed her chin and then buried his face in her sweet neck. "I know, baby, I know. But I promise it will just be for a day or two." Or three or four. He hoped it wasn't for long. As much as he loved Megan and wanted her to himself, he was discovering just how much he loved her family, too.

"Now," he said, pulling back, "we're supposed to pack a few toys."

"I did," Torie assured him, waving toward her bed.

He cleared his throat. "Little one, I think maybe

Grandma should've explained what few means. That means only, uh, five toys.''

"How many is five?"

He held up one hand, his fingers spread out. "This many. And that's all," he said, trying to sound stern.

After some negotiating, he grabbed a suitcase from his closet and packed Torie's choices. Then they joined Faith and Drew downstairs.

"Ready?" he asked.

She nodded, her throat working, as if she would cry.

"It's just for a few days, Faith. I promise."

She nodded and tried to smile.

"Are you sad, too, Grandma?" Torie asked.

"Yes, but we'll have fun, you know. Everything will be fine."

"I know. Daddy said so."

Torie's faith in his word filled Rick's heart. He hoped he never failed her. And he hoped she didn't discuss her trust with Megan.

He delivered Faith and the children to the Baxters, receiving assurances from Mabel and her husband Ed that they'd keep his family safe.

Then he headed back to the house. He had some calls to make, hoping he'd find some more men to work on the ranch. His promise to himself to make it on his own was forgotten. He had a family to protect, and he intended to use every resource he had to do so.

Fortunately he had a lot of resources.

Only one question remained.

Had Megan remembered she'd be alone on the ranch with him since Faith and the children had left?

Chapter Sixteen

It had struck Megan that she'd be alone at the ranch with Rick when she got in the car after work. Until then, her mind had been full with the notion of Drake Moody's possible appearance and the demands of her job.

She sat behind the wheel without starting the motor, staring into space. She'd tried to avoid thinking about Rick and his lies. But it had been impossible.

She'd counted herself lucky to find an honest man, an honorable man…and a man without wealth. Now she'd discovered he hadn't been honest, which wasn't honorable, and he had even more wealth than Drake.

And she was married to him.

In his defense, he'd never tried to manipulate her. He'd done his best to protect the children. And while he'd let her know he wanted her, she had been the one to initiate their lovemaking.

Wearily, she let out a long breath. So she couldn't blame him for the mess she was in. For falling in love with a man she didn't really know.

For making their marriage real without taking the time to be sure.

And her anger wasn't really with Rick. It was with herself. She'd made all those promises to herself, and she'd broken every one.

It was time to tell Rick the truth.

It was her fault that the marriage had gone as far as it had. She was sorry, she'd made a mistake. She'd give him a divorce as soon as he wanted it.

Without taking any money from him.

That had to be the reason he'd kept it all a secret. Like most people with money, he wanted to protect what was his.

She drove slowly home, wondering if Rick would continue the pretense long enough for her to get custody of the children. Or would he decide they weren't worth the effort? After all, he could hire a housekeeper if he wanted.

Though she'd hoped he would be at work, and she could postpone their conversation for a little longer, she found him waiting at the backdoor when she got out of her car.

His gaze burned into her, causing shivers on her arms, as she approached.

"Hi. I made some lunch, if you're hungry."

She swallowed. Lunch. Even if she managed to eat anything, she wasn't sure she could keep it down. "Um, thanks, but—"

"You didn't eat breakfast. Your mother and the kids made me promise I'd take care of you."

She avoided looking at him, but she couldn't help

poking fun at his words, just a little. "Yeah, I bet Drew was adamant that I eat lunch."

Rick chuckled slightly, surprising her. "Yeah, he threatened to arm wrestle me."

She looked at him, then, pleasure surging through her at his handsome face, a smile parting his lips. She looked away hurriedly.

"I'll eat something," she promised, going past him into the house.

He'd heated the leftovers from yesterday's lunch and had it waiting on the table, two places nicely set. What a change from that first dinner at his house.

She laid her purse on the kitchen cabinet and sat down, immediately taking a long sip of tea. Her throat felt as dry as dust.

Sitting down across from her, Rick picked up a dish and offered it to her. She took a little corn, then salad and a biscuit. He put a slice of meatloaf on her plate.

"I can serve myself," she insisted.

"I didn't figure you'd take enough. I don't want you passing out on me."

She didn't want that either. It would mean losing control.

"I talked to Mom before I left the office. She said the kids were settling in. Drew seemed to enjoy playing with Cal and Jessica's little boy."

"They're about the same age, aren't they?"

"Yes. Their son, Spence and Melanie's son, and

Alex and Tuck's little girl were all born on the same day, Samantha and Mac's wedding day.''

''Sounds like their wedding was even more exciting than ours.''

She didn't want to talk about their wedding day.

Finally she couldn't stand the silence any longer. ''Rick—''

At the same time he began, ''Megan—''

They both stopped and Megan risked a brief glance at his face. Then she quickly looked away.

''Megan, I owe you an apology.''

''No!'' she protested vehemently, surprising him. ''You don't. We had an agreement. Your private life isn't any of my business. We'll stick to the agreement, that and nothing else. Unless you're not willing to continue the bargain.''

''No! I mean—I want to continue—''

The phone rang.

She stood to go answer it and Rick caught her hand. ''Let it ring. We need to—''

''No. It might be Mom.''

When she reached the phone, trying to breathe deeply, she discovered it wasn't her mother, but Cal.

''Megan? I spread the word about anyone asking directions to the ranch. Leroy at the gas station called. A man just left after getting directions. I'm on my way, but I wanted you to be prepared in case it's Moody.''

''Thanks, Cal.''

''Is Rick there with you?''

"Yes."

"Okay, play it cool."

"We will."

She hung up the phone and stood there, one hand over her mouth.

She hadn't heard Rick move, but suddenly he was there, his hands on her shoulders.

"What is it?"

"It was Cal. A man asked directions. Cal thinks it might be Drake. He's on his way here."

"Cal or Drake?"

With a burst of hysterical laughter, she said, "Both. Looks like we're having company."

He squeezed her shoulders, but she didn't turn around. Finally, he muttered, "I'll clear the table."

At least he wasn't urging her to eat anymore. Which would've been useless.

She fixed another pitcher of tea. Maybe the cool liquid would help them stay cool, as Cal had ordered.

They sat in silence, waiting, listening to the ticking of the clock. Conversation about the weather would've been impossible at that moment, much less the serious discussion they'd been having when Cal called.

Besides, what else was there to discuss? Then she remembered. She hadn't told Rick she wouldn't take any of his money. That would be important to him.

But she'd fix that omission as soon as Drake had been routed.

The sound of a car turning into the drive made her stiffen her shoulders. Rick got up and moved to the kitchen window.

"It's Cal," he murmured. "He must've driven pretty fast."

He held open the backdoor as Cal approached. "Doing a little speeding?"

Cal grinned and said, "Police business."

Megan hadn't moved, and she didn't acknowledge Cal's arrival until he greeted her. Then she nodded.

"I passed him on the way, Megan. He's a blonde, about mid-thirties. Does that sound right?"

"Yes," she said with a sigh. "Torie got her blond hair from him."

Another car turned into their drive and Megan closed her eyes. She wasn't worried about her physical safety. Rick and Cal were big and strong. She knew they'd both protect her.

It was Drake's ugliness, inside him, and the horrible memories he brought with him, that disturbed her. The regrets and anger for the waste of her sister's life.

"He's going to the front door," Rick said. He started in that direction.

"I'll answer the door," Megan said, rising, calm settling over her.

Rick frowned at her. "No. There's no need—"

"There's every need," Megan assured him. "I won't have that man thinking I'm afraid of him."

Cal nodded and rewarded Megan with a smile.

"That-a-girl! Bullies like to smell fear. And we'll be right behind you."

"I know you will," she told him, thanking him with her smile.

Rick held open the door and she passed by him just as the knock sounded. When she swung open the front door, girded for battle, the air suddenly rushed out of her.

"Mr. Astin, I'm a reporter from Austin. I wondered if I could have a few words with you?"

Megan stared at the man who had rushed into speech before any of them could speak.

It wasn't Drake Moody.

That thought was all her mind could hold at the moment.

It wasn't Drake Moody.

Then the realization hit her that she'd have to go through her fears until it *was* him. The worry and tension wouldn't go away. Not yet.

Tears pooled in her eyes and she stumbled back, away from the door.

"Megan—" Rick called, reaching for her.

"Mr. Astin, please—" the reporter pleaded.

"You deal with him. I'll see about Megan," Cal told him and followed her as she hurried back to the kitchen.

RICK DIDN'T want to deal with the reporter.

Hell! Now that he'd been found, he was going to have to build a gate to keep them out. A posted gate, with an electric fence.

But most of all, he wanted to be at Megan's side, supporting her, comforting her.

Instead, he had to talk to this stranger. But he knew better than to blow him off. He'd only come back again with others following him. He gave him five minutes of rapid-fire questions and answers, then showed him out.

When he entered the kitchen, he discovered Cal sitting in his place across from Megan, both of them having a glass of iced tea.

"Megan, are you all right?"

"Yes, of course."

Her calm both pleased and irritated him. He'd wanted to be the one for her to lean on. "Okay, then how about eating your lunch."

"You haven't eaten yet?" Cal asked, lifting his eyebrows. "It's almost two o'clock."

"And she skipped breakfast," Rick added.

"Fine!" she snapped. "I'll eat lunch, but I'm not a child. You don't have to hover over me."

"Yes, ma'am," he agreed as he removed her plate from the refrigerator and put it in the microwave. "How about you, Cal? Can I interest you in a meatloaf sandwich?"

"Is it the meatloaf from yesterday?" the sheriff asked. At Rick's nod, he said enthusiastically, "You bet."

"You haven't had lunch either?" Megan asked, surprised.

Cal looked sheepish. "Yeah, I have, but I'm still hungry."

For the first time since Cal called, she smiled. "I've heard that line before."

Rick fixed Cal's sandwich and warmed up his own plate. Then he sat down beside Megan. He wanted to finish their discussion, to convince her things couldn't be like they were. They couldn't go back to an agreement, a bare, unemotional business arrangement.

Not when they'd shared a bed.

Not when he loved her.

Not when she and Faith and the children were his family.

Half an hour later, Cal left. Rick thanked him for the warning and for coming out. He promised to let Mac know what had happened, and to call if there were any more alarms.

After seeing him to the door, Rick shut it and turned to face Megan.

"I've finished," she hurriedly said, standing to take her plate to the sink.

She'd eaten a little, but he wasn't going to insist she eat any more. He was, however, going to insist that she not run away and hide, as it appeared she intended to do.

"Fine," he said calmly, coming toward her. "Then we can continue our discussion."

"I've finished our discussion. Except to tell you I won't take any of your precious money. We'll pay our way if you'll let the marriage stand until the custody hearing. But we can move out, if that's what you want."

"You have no idea what I want."

She lifted her chin at those words, her jaw squaring. Rick almost smiled at the sign that he'd riled her. Anything was better than that cold calmness she'd shown earlier.

"I think I do. You didn't tell me about the money because you were afraid I'd ask for a settlement in the divorce."

"I didn't know there'd be a divorce when we made our agreement, did I?"

"No, but that's why you didn't say anything, isn't it? You hadn't told anyone in Cactus."

"It wasn't their business," he assured her, taking a step closer, which he noted made her nervous.

"It isn't mine, either. You've done me a favor, and I hope we've paid you back with good housekeeping. That's all that's involved."

"I don't think so. What about the other night?" He didn't bother specifying which night. He knew they both would never forget it.

She licked her lips and looked away. Then, with the courage she'd already shown, she faced him. "That was a mistake, one that won't be repeated."

"A mistake? It was the most glorious night of my life," he said softly, coming one step closer.

Pain lanced through her eyes and she closed them briefly.

"Megan, I love you. I wanted to tell you then, but I was a little distracted at the time. Afterward, you passed out on me. I didn't want to wake you the next morning because you hadn't gotten much sleep, but—"

"Please, Rick, this isn't necessary. I told you I wouldn't take your money. I'm not your ex-wife. I'm not going to sue for half your fortune."

"You want my money, it's yours."

She almost screamed. "I told you I didn't want it! Okay? Is that clear? Your money isn't important to me!"

He grinned. "I know."

"Then why do you keep offering it to me?" she demanded, irritation in her voice.

"Because it isn't important to me, either."

That silenced her. She didn't even protest when he pulled her against him, wrapping his arms around her for the first time since he'd loved her. He closed his eyes, savoring the feel of her.

Before he'd got his fill of holding her, as if he ever would, she pushed back. "But—"

"Do you remember someone saying money wasn't important? It was what you could do with it that mattered? Do you remember all those ideas you had?"

She nodded, looking puzzled.

"Well, we can do all those things. And we can add on to the house, so there's enough room for all of us…and any other children that come along. And we can be happy. If you'll let us."

"Me?"

"You. You're the key to everything, Megan. I love you with all my heart. I want us to be together until the end of time. But I don't want to force you. I don't want to buy you. I want you to *choose* me. To commit yourself to me, as I'm committing myself to you.''

Megan leaned back and drew a deep breath. She'd come to the crossroads with an important choice to make. She'd promised herself she would never be in her sister's shoes.

Rick had lied to her. He had hidden something from her. But he wasn't Drake Moody. He was a good man, and he loved her. With a sigh, she smiled.

''I choose you, Rick Astin, as long as you understand that I come with some baggage. Namely, Faith, Torie and Drew.''

Almost as she finished her last words, Rick's lips covered her in a soul-searing kiss, made even more stunning by the promise in his touch.

When he finally raised his head, he whispered, ''I wouldn't have it any other way.''

Megan beamed at him. ''You know, I made the best wedding bargain ever when I asked you to marry me.''

Rick frowned. ''I'm worried our children will think I'm a wimp when they hear that *you* proposed to *me*.''

''I even seduced you,'' she added, a saucy grin on her lips that made him kiss her again.

''Hmm, I'm going to have to think of a way to prove my manhood,'' he whispered, his lips traveling to her neck.

"I think—"

The phone rang again.

"Damn it, won't anybody leave us alone?" Rick exclaimed.

Megan left his embrace and answered the phone, grinning at him over her shoulder.

Mac was calling. "Megan, I have some news for you."

She flashed a look at Rick that brought him to her side, his arms going around her.

"What is it?"

"Drake Moody is dead."

She gasped and Rick took the phone from her ear. "What did you say?"

"Rick, Drake Moody is dead."

"What? How?"

"Apparently he was celebrating his release and got drunk. He hit a tree going ninety miles an hour."

"So it's all over?"

"Yeah. I don't think his parents will sue for custody."

"No, I don't, either. Thanks for calling, Mac."

He repeated the conversation for Megan's benefit.

"Are you okay?"

"Yes." She breathed a deep sigh. "So all our worry was for nothing. We didn't need to move here. I didn't have to marry you. It was all for nothing."

Rick's heart stopped. "Megan—"

Her arms went around his neck and a brilliant smile lit up her face. "I'm the luckiest woman in the world!"

Still worried, he asked, "Because you'll have custody of the kids?"

"That, of course, but...but I found you. I found my belief in love and marriage. I found happiness. If I hadn't come here and done those things, I'd still be an angry, bitter woman in Fort Worth." Something about his stillness must have alarmed her. "You do still want me, don't you?"

He gave her a kiss that knocked her socks off. "Want you? I'll always want and love you, sweetheart. And I'm going to prove it to you right now."

He swept her into his arms and started up the stairs.

"But I should call Mom and let her know she can come home. I mean, here."

"You had the right word. This is home, for all of us. But we're going to have a couple of hours of honeymoon first, wife. We've earned it. And I can't wait any longer."

Megan convinced him of her agreement without speaking a word.

Epilogue

"Megan, Rick called me about the child care program!" Samantha said, as Megan entered her office a month later. "I'm so excited about it."

Smiling, Megan agreed that it was wonderful.

"And I heard he's putting computers in the schools. He's even starting a company right here in Cactus. He's doing all those things we talked about at dinner that night."

"I know. He's wonderful, isn't he?" Her contented smile told Samantha she believed her words.

"Yes, he is, but don't tell Mac I said that. He might get jealous," she warned with a chuckle.

Megan laughed, too.

"Everything's turned out so well. I'm glad for both of you," Samantha said. "All you need now is a baby on the way, and you'll be as happy as me."

Megan continued to smile. "That's why I'm early. I think we'd better run a test."

Samantha sprang to her feet, which wasn't easy

since she was getting bigger every day. "A test? You mean you think you're pregnant?"

"Yes. I think I'm pregnant." She was pretty sure, actually. And she suspected she got that way the first night she and Rick made love.

A few minutes later, she was proved right.

"Is Rick going to be happy?" Samantha asked. "After all, you already have your sister's children."

"He'll be thrilled. But meet us at dinner tonight at The Last Roundup and you can ask him yourself. Cal and Jessica, Tuck and Alex and Spence and Melanie are coming. We're going to celebrate our good fortune and thank all of you for your support."

"Wonderful! When are you going to tell Rick?"

"As soon as I get home from work."

A few hours later, she reached the house. Though she'd suspected her pregnancy, she hadn't said a word to Rick. She wanted to be sure before she told him.

"Where's Rick?" she asked her mother as she entered.

"I believe he went to the barn to talk to Jose," Faith said. She was putting dishes in the dishwasher.

"Are the kids down for their naps?"

"Yes, though Torie protested. She thinks she's getting too old for a nap." Faith sighed. "The only way I got her to lie down was to tell her Flower was a growing dog and needed her rest. They're in bed together."

Megan grinned. When she'd been a child, her mother hadn't wanted any pets in the house. How things had changed in a glorious, wonderful way.

"I'll be back in a minute."

She hurried to the barn. Rick had hired Jose as his foreman, upping his pay considerably, so he could quit and manage his own place sooner. Now there were several men to work under Jose.

Rick had combined ranching with a return to business that gave him the best of two worlds. And a lot of time to spend with his family.

And making love to her.

"Rick?" she called as she entered the barn.

"Back here, Meg," he called and she heard his boots as he hurried to meet her.

Even with Jose behind him, he swept her into his arms for a mind-blowing kiss. "You're home," he murmured into her ears. "Hang on a second, and I'll be free."

She smiled and he finished giving directions to Jose, his arm wrapped around her.

Jose, after nodding to her, left the barn, and Rick turned his attention completely to her. "Want to go take a nap?" His suggestive grin told her what he had in mind.

"Mmm, yes. Samantha suggested I take a nap."

"Really? Were you sleepy at the office? I didn't think we stayed up too late last night."

"We didn't, but in my condition—"

She waited for the other shoe to drop. It didn't take long.

"You're pregnant? Really?" He whooped and lifted her into his arms, spinning around.

When he finally put her down, she asked, "Why are you surprised? You've been working on it ever since that first night."

His cheeks flamed. "You figured that out?"

"Yes, I did."

"I know I should've protected you, but…but you were giving yourself to me. I figured we were committed to each other, and…and I wanted you to carry my child." He cleared his throat. "But it was instinctive, not planned. I wasn't trying to force you into anything. Are you happy about the baby?"

She loved his frown, his loving concern. He was naturally bossy, but she was keeping him on his toes. And she wanted this baby as much as he did.

Their family was going to grow.

But that would only make life better.

"Oh, yes, I'm happy."

In Rick's arms, she always would be.   ✕

*Be sure to return to the town of Cactus
when Judy Christenberry's*
TOTS FOR TEXAS *series
continues in September— only from
Harlequin American Romance.*

If you enjoyed what you just read,
then we've got an offer you can't resist!

Take 2 bestselling love stories FREE!
Plus get a FREE surprise gift!

Clip this page and mail it to Harlequin Reader Service®

IN U.S.A.	IN CANADA
3010 Walden Ave.	P.O. Box 609
P.O. Box 1867	Fort Erie, Ontario
Buffalo, N.Y. 14240-1867	L2A 5X3

YES! Please send me 2 free Harlequin American Romance® novels and my free surprise gift. Then send me 4 brand-new novels every month, which I will receive months before they're available in stores. In the U.S.A., bill me at the bargain price of $3.57 plus 25¢ delivery per book and applicable sales tax, if any*. In Canada, bill me at the bargain price of $3.96 plus 25¢ delivery per book and applicable taxes**. That's the complete price and a savings of at least 10% off the cover prices—what a great deal! I understand that accepting the 2 free books and gift places me under no obligation ever to buy any books. I can always return a shipment and cancel at any time. Even if I never buy another book from Harlequin, the 2 free books and gift are mine to keep forever. So why not take us up on our invitation. You'll be glad you did!

154 HEN C22W
354 HEN C22X

Name	(PLEASE PRINT)	
Address	Apt.#	
City	State/Prov.	Zip/Postal Code

* Terms and prices subject to change without notice. Sales tax applicable in N.Y.
** Canadian residents will be charged applicable provincial taxes and GST.
  All orders subject to approval. Offer limited to one per household.
  ® are registered trademarks of Harlequin Enterprises Limited.

AMER00   ©1998 Harlequin Enterprises Limited